MW01234588

T

by

Chasity Bowlin

ALSO BY CHASITY BOWLIN

The Dark Regency Series, VOL I

The Haunting of a Duke
The Redemption of a Rogue
The Enticement of an Earl

Standalone Titles

The Beast of Bath
The Last Offer

The Dark Regency Series, VOL II

A Love So Dark
A Passion So Strong
A Heart So Wicked (coming soon)

Dedication

To everyone who loves a fairytale.

PROLOGUE
Grantham, 1816

Algernon Dunne entered the Angel and Royal Inn in the wee hours of the morning. Patrons slept on the floor of the tap room, snoring softly from exhaustion or excess. The innkeeper whom he'd roused glared at him.

He had no patience for the man's short temper and little inclination to deal with it. As always, coin was the most expedient method to smooth his way. "Lord Holland has a room here. Direct me to it."

The innkeeper shook his head, "I'll send up a maid so as not to disturb the lady."

Algernon placed another coin with the first. "There's no need. The key, if you please."

The innkeeper produced a key and passed it to him. "Get your business done and get gone, the lot of you. I don't know what either one of you is about but that girl isn't his wife, and she's not well. I'll not have some gently bred girl dying in my inn and ruining my business."

"What a compassionate soul you are," Algernon

said dryly as he turned toward the narrow stairs.

"The room is the last one at the end of the hall," the innkeeper said, and his tone was just as cool as before.

Climbing the stairs slowly, Algernon had no idea what he would find when he opened that door. Whatever lay beyond, he knew that their lives would all be changed irrevocably by it.

Fitting the key into the lock, the well oiled mechanism turned soundlessly. The innkeeper might lack compassion, but he was clearly diligent about the maintenance of his property.

The door swung inward with a soft whoosh. There was just enough light streaming through the windows to illuminate the couple lying on the bed. There was no mistaking it for an intimate encounter. The man was clothed, lying atop the covers, watching the pale and wan face of the woman as if every breath might be her last.

"What happened?" Algernon demanded softly.

"Melville's drunkard of a coachman sent them into the river," came the soft reply, nearly a whisper. "The coachman is dead. Melville as well. But Olivia survived for the simple fact that Melville had bound her hands and secured them to a hook inside the carriage... Otherwise, she would have drowned with them. The impact dislocated her shoulder. I helped the doctor to set it earlier."

Algernon's heart thundered in his chest. She was his only family, all that he had left. And he'd very nearly lost her. "You need to leave, Burke. Before anyone discovers you here."

Lord Burke Holland rose from the bed and glared at him. "Then I'll take my leave before my presence sullies her any further... But you need to ask yourself, Algernon, what part you played in this near tragedy."

"What part I played?" he demanded, outraged at the accusation. "I would never have allowed Melville near her. Olivia was reckless and she very nearly paid the ultimate price for it!"

"Not reckless," Burke corrected him. "Desperate. Lonely. Vulnerable because of your damnable pride."

The words stung, primarily because they were true. But Algernon was having none of it. Those were admissions he was unwilling to make. "You've gone too far."

Burke continued. "You're so puffed up with your own circumstance you can't see that you've made her life a misery.... she's just something else you put on display to show the world how far above everyone you are. But she's not a piece of art, or a priceless artifact. She's a flesh and blood woman denied her own life for far too long."

The fury that accusation elicited in him was fueled by guilt. "I've denied her nothing! You're the one who feels denied... Should I have granted you permission to court her then? To ply her with trinkets and romantic gestures until she agreed to wed you?"

"I love her! I have loved her for years and would do anything to make her happy!"

Algernon was beyond furious, beyond caring that the words escaping him would destroy a man he'd called friend, a man who'd risked everything to save his sister from an opportunist. "You're no better than Melville. What do you have to offer her? A tattered reputation, a family full or miscreants and a family seat that's crumbling around your ears? You claim to love her... but she'd never be sure, would she, Burke? There would always be the question of whether you loved her or money!"

Burke flew at him then, taking him to the ground. The fist that landed on his jaw was like steel, the impact of it jarring through him. Burke was heavier, larger, but Algernon fought back, landing several staggering blows of his own. They grappled, both men in a fit of fury and temper.

They were both bloodied and winded, but neither was giving ground. It was only the soft cry from the bed, a sound of pain and distress that caused the men to break apart.

Burke rose and moved toward the bed, but Algernon was having none of it. "It isn't your place to tend to her," he said sharply.

Burke stopped, halting mid stride. He snapped over his shoulder at Algernon, "Go to hell." But he made no move to approach the bed. Instead he grabbed his greatcoat where it had been discarded and stormed out into the night.

Algernon moved closer to the bed just as Olivia opened her eyes. Even in the dim light, he could see the dark bruise on her forehead and the numerous scrapes and bruises that accompanied it. Her right arm was bound to her chest

"Burke," she whispered.

"He's gone, Livi," Algernon said softly.

"Melville's dead," she whispered. "He's dead and I'm glad. I'm a horrible person."

"Nonsense," he reassured her. There was a bottle on the table that was obviously laudanum. Reaching for it, he placed several drops in a glass and pressed it to her lips. "Go to sleep, Liv. It'll all look better tomorrow."

Chapter One
1817

As morning sun streamed into the breakfast room of the Dunne townhouse in Mayfair, Olivia sat to her brother's left as he perused the morning paper. The slip of paper tucked into the sleeve of her morning gown was like a leaden weight. It was not a conversation she looked forward to, but it was necessary.

Taking a deep breath, she plunged ahead. "Algernon, I've been thinking that I should like to move to a house of my own."

His surprise was apparent in the cool arching of one brow. "Why would you wish to leave your home?" he asked, reaching for his coffee cup. The bitter drink had become a morning ritual for him.

She would shock him. Quite possibly, what she had to tell him would infuriate him, but she'd learned the hard way how dangerous it was to keep secrets from her brother. Memories long buried stirred in her, of Melville and his ham handed attempt to abduct her to Scotland for an elopement. Memories of the pain and fear afterward, of seeing Melville's lifeless body bobbing in the water that poured into the carriage after the crash. After that, it all became vague and fuzzy, details lost in a haze of pain and laudanum.

Disturbed by her own thoughts, she spoke as matter-of-factly as her nerves and embarrassment would permit. "I've decided to take a lover."

Algernon choked on the coffee he had just sipped—his face red and his eyes tearing up as he sputtered. When at last he could breathe again, he demanded, "What the devil has gotten into you, Olivia? That is impossible!"

"Algie," she said, reverting to the childhood nickname that only she was permitted to use for him, "We both know that I will not marry... Not now. My reputation is far beyond salvage and any offers that might come are for old men seeking nurses or young hot heads seeking my fortune. I may have fallen, but my standards have not. I want no part of either but that doesn't mean I am ready to enter a nunnery."

She'd known that her words, at least at first, would

not sway him. She was also certain that if she persevered, he would come around. So she allowed him his protest.

His tone was strident and quite firm. "First, you are an unmarried woman and cannot possibly live alone. Second, regardless of your reputation, you and I both know that you are entirely innocent. While there are women in this world, in far worse situations than yours, who give their bodies without giving their hearts, you are not one of them. You will be heartbroken by this foolishness."

Olivia sighed as she began countering the arguments. She'd come fully prepared for all of them. "I'm not innocent, Algernon. I may be a virgin, but I am not innocent. Not now. Innocence implies that I have no notion of how cruel the world can be, and that is no longer true. As to being heartbroken, I would rather have my heart broken than allow it to simply wither in my chest…Is it so very wrong to want passion in my life? To feel something other than the dreaded monotony of getting up every morning to have every day be exactly the same?"

Algernon started to speak, but she held up her hand and continued. As she spoke, her voice rose unintentionally.

Shouting was not something that Olivia Dunne did. She was always calm, always circumspect, and her behavior always proper, but propriety had failed her utterly and left her miserable. "I wake up. We have breakfast. You leave to take care of business or go to your clubs or go to your mistress—and please don't mistake that I am blissfully unaware—and I sit here. There are no callers. No one will be seen coming into this house to visit me."

She stood up abruptly, her chair nearly tipping backward, and began to pace the room as she continued, "Then I sort through the mail, and the painfully thin stack of invitations that we receive… well, the painfully thin stack that is addressed to us *both*. After that, I have lunch. Then I sit. Then I have tea. Then I sit. Then we have supper, and possibly, we go out to a party or a ball afterward, where I will go, and I will *sit*, because even though I have been invited as a courtesy to you, I am not really welcome. No one will talk to me, no one will dance with me, unless it is some aging roué who thinks I am up for grabs or some grasping fortune hunter who thinks I am desperate for a husband."

When she had finished, Olivia returned to her chair and seated herself. Other than her slightly flushed face, there was no indication that she had just ranted like a madwoman or shouted at her brother like a fishwife.

Concern was etched on Algernon's face. He looked at her as if she were some fragile thing ready to topple and shatter. "I will stay at home more. We will spend more time together. I have been horribly selfish in leaving you alone so much—." His offer was interrupted by the smashing of dishes.

The breakfast plate that had been sitting before Olivia was now lying in shattered pieces on the opposite side of the room. Surprised, she wasn't quite sure how it had happened. Surely, she *must* have thrown it, though such a display was entirely unlike her. Of course, she was arguing with her elder brother about her right to take a lover. Many things about the morning were quite unlike her.

"You can't possibly understand!" she said, her voice trembling with frustration and pent up anger. "I don't want you to give up your life. I want to build one of my *own!* No, it won't be the one that had been envisioned for me.

Marriage, a family… that is gone. But I can have friends and I can have a lover, if I accept that my place in society now is no longer the place in society that I was born to… You need to live *your* life, Algie. You need to find a wife, and you will not do that as long as I am in this house. No respectable woman will live here while I am in residence. Had it not been for me, you would have married already!"

He opened his mouth to protest, but the words to make it all go away simply did not exist. This wasn't the skinned knee of her childhood, or the slight of a vicious girl. Those small hurts he'd soothed easily enough. This was something altogether different. "Olivia—"

She held up her hand, stemming his protests. "My reputation, Algie, is already in tatters. It has been for the better part of the past year. I am, in the eyes of the ton, well and truly ruined."

It was a fact he would not be able to argue. Her reputation was beyond repair though it was through no fault of her own. Still, taking a lover was not an endeavor typically undertaken by young ladies of breeding.

"And if I forbid it, Liv?" he asked softly.

She didn't flinch, nor did she relent. Instead, she looked him directly in the eye and said with a resolve that rang with conviction, "I was not asking for your permission, Algernon. I was merely informing you of my plans. I am twenty-five years old and will come into my own fortune soon enough. I have no marital prospects to speak of, certainly none that I would ever consider. The world already believes me to be a woman who played fast and loose with her virtue… Should I not have the benefit of actually experiencing what the world has already condemned of me?"

It was an argument that could not be easily refuted, though he persevered. "Marriage is not entirely out of the question for you, Olivia. There have been offers since the scandal broke… But if you do this, even those offers will be withdrawn."

She snorted, a very unladylike sound that would never have escaped her only a year earlier. Much had changed in her behavior and her attitude since then. "Yes, my wondrous offers of marriage. Old men who could never hope to be an actual husband and men who desire my fortune so much that my alleged lack of virtue is utterly unimportant to them… I will not be a nurse to a dying bridegroom, nor will I be a walking banknote for men who have already squandered their own fortunes."

There had been three offers in fact. Two of them had been from men well into their dotage and one had been from a man on the verge of being tossed into debtor's prison. He tried a different tack. "You still have a place in society," he argued. "You are still invited to parties and balls. If you proceed with this ridiculous plan, those invitations will cease and you will be a pariah. What then?"

Olivia favored him with a baleful stare. "I hadn't planned, brother dear, to openly become someone's mistress. It *is* possible to have a lover and be discreet. You've managed it frequently enough over the years… I intend to do this, Algernon. Nothing you can say will dissuade me. If you are truly so worried about what remains of my tattered reputation, then you will help me with my list of suitable prospects."

He took another sip of coffee. It was clear from his stubborn expression that he was simply willing the situation to just go away, as if she couldn't be serious about it. But they were both well aware that she was. Olivia did not jest. In fact, she hadn't truly laughed or smiled in the last year.

"You wish me, your brother, to help you select a lover?" he asked, incredulously.

She rolled her eyes. "When you put it that way, it does sound very strange, indeed. As to selecting a lover, no, I will do that for myself. What I wish from you is to review my list of prospects and tell me if the gentlemen I am considering can be trusted to be discreet...or if there are things about them to which I am not privy that would make them unsuitable. I am asking you to help me reduce the threat of discovery."

Algernon knew that he was thoroughly caught in this snare of hers. If he didn't review her list, she would simply proceed without his assistance and almost assuredly worsen her already difficult situation. If he did help her, he was essentially giving her his blessing to engage in an affair. It was an impossible situation. "Olivia, I wish that you would reconsider... Regardless of what the rest of society believes, you and I both know that you are still an innocent.

If you embark upon this path, there is no turning back."

The stare that she leveled at him was filled with world weary wisdom and a healthy amount of pity. "Will you review the list?"

He was damned, he thought. He was utterly damned. "Yes, I will review your list."

Olivia smiled at him then. Her face lost the tension that had been her constant companion for the past year, and she looked lovelier and more carefree than he had seen her in some time. He had allowed himself to forget how unhappy she was. No. He had deliberately chosen to ignore her unhappiness, he thought. Ignoring it meant that he could also ignore his guilt in bringing about her misery. Had he chosen a husband for her years earlier, or even given serious consideration to any of the reasonable offers that he had received for her hand over the years, she would never have been in the position to be Melville's victim. She would have been wed, with a home of her own, and possibly a child. His own vanity and pride in believing that no man was good enough for his sister had marked her as a target for a true villain. Burke's accusations of a year ago came back to him, along with the awful, sinking feeling that the other man had been correct on all counts. "I am sorry, Liv that it has come to this… I should have been a better guardian. If I had—." He stopped, unable even then to admit his guilt aloud.

Olivia did not speak for several moments. "If any of the gentlemen that had offered for me over the years had held even the slightest bit of interest for me, do you think I would not have interceded? Do you really believe that if I had wanted to marry one of them that I would have allowed you to so summarily refuse them?"

She would not have, of course. He knew her well enough to know that Olivia was not shy about expressing what she wanted. She had been getting her way since she was a small child. "Where is this list?"

Olivia produced a folded slip of paper that had been tucked into the sleeve of her morning dress and slid it across the surface of the table toward his outstretched hand. Outwardly, she appeared calm, but he knew it was a ruse.

The list was short. There were only four names on it. Two could be eliminated outright. "Briarleigh is out," he said. "He just married Miss Emmaline Walters in the midst of a scandal. Ellersleigh is out as well. He's rumored to have wed, as well... and Wright is definitely not the one."

Her eyes narrowed and she looked at him with suspicion. "Are you dismissing my choices because you think it will prevent me from forging ahead with my plan?"

She had every right to suspect him of it, but in that instance he was innocent. "No, I am not. Wright would not be interested in affair with you, Liv. He prefers boys... very young boys. It isn't common knowledge but suffice to say I discovered him in a very compromising situation one evening that leaves little doubt as to his preferences."

The last and final name on the list had been written once, crossed out, and then added again. Lord Burke, Viscount Holland. He read it a second time, just to be sure. It appeared his sins were coming back to haunt him.

"Burke is on your list?" he asked, keeping his tone perfectly neutral.

Olivia nodded. "I realize that your friendship with Viscount Holland has cooled over the past years, but I thought I could count on him to be discreet."

She could. Algernon didn't question it. Burke would never do anything to harm Olivia, of that he was completely certain. He also didn't think Burke would agree to dishonor his sister. Regardless, if Olivia pursued an affair with him, the ugliness was bound to come out. "Why did you cross him out initially?"

Olivia shrugged. "I have known him for so long, and yet he never displayed any signs of attraction. I am not certain that he would be interested in embarking upon an affair with me."

It wasn't lack of interest that would keep Burke away. It was an unimpeachable sense of honor and copious amounts of pride. Algernon considered his options and knew within an instant that there was only one course for him. "If you could marry, Olivia, if there was a chance that you could marry a man who had genuine feeling for you and not your inheritance, would you?"

She laughed, but the sound was mirthless. It was hard and bitter. "Of course, I would. That was all I ever wanted, at any rate. But we both know that is no longer a possibility for me. Gentlemen do not marry women with reputations like mine, regardless of whether or not it was earned."

Had there ever been a decision for him to make at all, he wondered? It appeared that fate was intervening to right old wrongs. "From this list, Holland is your only candidate."

Olivia nodded. "We've been invited to the Somerfield Ball tomorrow night, but I have not accepted yet. Is he likely to attend?"

He would. Algernon would be certain of it. He would lend fate a hand for a change, rather than attempt to thwart it. "I think so… Send our acceptance to Lord and Lady Somerfield. I shall escort you."

"You do not plan to sabotage this for me?" she demanded. She knew him well, and knew that he could be both sneaky and underhanded when it served his purposes.

He shook his head. "No. I wish that I could change your mind, persuade you to reconsider, but I will not intentionally attempt to inhibit your pursuit…I just wish that I knew why you were doing this. Why now?"

Olivia sighed. The sound carried a wealth of sadness. It was difficult to explain something she did not understand herself. It had been more than a year since the abduction, since the events had unfolded that had led to her public ruin. In that time, she had grown more and more isolated. She still attended the events, but her place within them had changed dramatically. She had lost her chance for love, for marriage and a family of her own. Panic had begun to set in.

She was still living a perfectly proper life, and she knew, that no matter how properly she behaved, or how contrite she appeared for something that had never been her fault anyway, society would never forgive her. She had come to feel that life was passing her by. If the world believed her to be whore, to have indulged her every carnal desire, what more could they do to her if she actually *did* indulge them? To answer her brother's question, she said, "The only thing that prevents young women from indulging their own desires for passion is the threat of losing one's reputation… mine is already lost. Therefore, there is nothing left for me to lose."

"Except your virginity," he said bluntly. They were

beyond the point of speaking politely.

"Virginity only has value when you can gift it to a husband. I never will," she said with a shrug. With that, she rose and left the breakfast room and left him staring after her wondering what position in hell he had just purchased for himself.

Chapter Two

Lord Burke, Viscount Holland, was seated at his usual table at White's. He was awaiting his lunch and considering what to do about a matter of some urgency at one of his estates. In reviewing the account books for one of his properties, his man of affairs had uncovered some disturbing figures. Ugly suspicions had come to light regarding the credibility of his steward's account keeping. There were glaring discrepancies in the books, indicating the man was incompetent or that he was a thief. Burke judged the latter to be a more likely explanation.

"Good afternoon, Holland."

Looking up, Burke met a clear, blue gaze that was incredibly familiar to him. Though it had been nearly a year since they had spoken, he had recognized Algernon Dunne's voice immediately. Burke didn't allow his surprise to show. His only response was to raise one peaked, black brow. "Dunne," he acknowledged coolly.

Algernon didn't wait for an invitation to join him, since it was clear none would be forthcoming. Instead, he simply seated himself as if it were entirely within his rights to do so. "You're looking quite well, these days. Clean living appears to be paying off for you."

Beneath the table, Burke's hands were tightly clenched as he battled the urge to smash his fist into Algernon's already large nose. "Indeed. One can only drink and carouse for so long before it begins to take a toll. Luckily, I chose to give it up before too much damage had been done... You'll forgive me for asking, but what the bloody hell do you want?"

Algernon smiled. Burke's impatience with drivel and small talk had always been one of the qualities he admired most in his friend. "I am here to atone for my sins. Tell me Holland, do they serve humble pie at White's?"

Burke sneered. "You've never been humble a day in your life."

"That isn't true. I was humbled the day Olivia was abducted. I was even more humbled when I had to beg your assistance in rescuing her...and then I became suitably enraged when Lady Haversham began her campaign to single handedly inform every man, woman and child in England that my sister had been ruined."

He should have called. Regardless of what had transpired in the past, following Olivia's difficulties he should have called on her and offered his support. "I trust that Olivia is well?" he said. He knew that she was. He had seen her at the Whitmore Ball only a week earlier, though he'd taken pains to ensure she did not see him. She was as alarmingly beautiful as ever, with her red-gold hair and bright blue eyes. She was no longer the belle of the ball, however. Rather than being surrounded by a cadre of admirers and dancing every single dance, she spent most of her time alone, or talking with other women who skirted the thin border between respectability and ruin.

Algernon considered his answer carefully, but in the end, elected to be as blunt as Burke would have been under those same circumstances. "She is quite well. She informed me at breakfast that she intends to take a lover."

There was no visible response to the statement. In spite of that, the tension emanating from Burke became a tangible thing. He was like a caged lion at that moment, a wild beast, barely contained. It might have been seconds before he replied or it could have been infinitely longer. When he did respond, he could only ask, "And you intend to permit this?"

"No one *permits* Olivia to do anything. Olivia has always done precisely as she wished, and until this moment, she had always wished to be proper and abide by the rules of society that bind all unmarried, young women. Now, she has decided not to," Algernon offered with a shrug. He added with a familiarity born of their long acquaintance, "And, as you well know, there is no power on earth that will stop her."

Burke felt there was a darkness growing within him, swirling, ugly and angry. He knew it for what it was. *Jealousy*. The very idea of another man putting his hands on Olivia made him want to smash things, but he did not. Calmly and with utter conviction, he stated, "I hope she doesn't become overly attached to him, because I will see him dead."

"That might be difficult…certainly imprudent. The man she has selected is you."

If he had been told that the sky was yellow and the

grass was purple, he wouldn't have been more taken aback. Olivia wished to take him as a lover. "Why are you telling me this? Have you become your sister's procurer, then?"

Algernon laughed. "I knew you would be mightily offended… and no, I have not become her procurer. I simply wanted to clear the air between us, and resolve some old issues. Otherwise, this could end badly for everyone."

Burke shook his head. "It will not end, because it will not begin. I would never dishonor her by making her my mistress. It is preposterous."

It was time to tell the truth, Algernon thought. The time for stalling was at an end. "Have you wondered why she would refuse your offer to court her three years ago and suddenly has decided that now she wishes to enter into an entirely different sort of relationship with you?"

Burke *had* wondered, but he wouldn't ask. He had never acknowledged to anyone that she had turned him away. It was both painful and utterly humiliating to have been rejected out of hand by a woman he had admired greatly and desired even more. "If you would get to the point, Dunne, it would be much appreciated."

Algernon leaned forward, resting his hands on the table and spoke softly. "Olivia never turned down your suit, because I never presented it to her."

It was not what he'd expected to hear. But in retrospect, did not surprise him one whit. Arrogant. High handed. Ruthless. Algernon Dunne was all those things and more. "Bastard."

Dunne took no offense to the epithet, but inclined his head in agreement. "Indeed. I behaved like a pompous, gloating ass. If you wish to pummel me beyond recognition, I will make no effort to stop you… but first, at least do me—and Olivia— the service, of hearing me out."

"Then speak your piece and do it quickly," Burke said. He was going to beat the man within an inch of his life and he was going to enjoy every second of it.

Algernon signaled one of the servants and ordered a bottle of brandy. Barely a moment had passed before the man returned with a bottle and two snifters. He poured a healthy amount into both glasses. "It isn't something that I am proud of. I behaved abominably to you both…In my defense, I was worried that you were not as reformed as you appeared to be, and that you would break my sister's heart."

"I would never do anything to harm, Olivia!"

"Shall I finish, or do you want to continue your protestations of love?"

Burke nodded abruptly.

Algernon continued, "I was also concerned about your finances, which were still a bit rocky then, and even more concerned about the scandals that your family seems to find like fleas on a dog. Additionally, Olivia had just made quite an impression on Prince Mikhail while he was visiting from Monte Negro. I thought he might actually offer for her... It wasn't that I wanted her to marry him, but that I wanted her to have that option."

"You wanted the prestige of having your sister courted by a prince," Burke said succinctly. Algernon had ever been prideful. His pride and vanity had gotten him into more trouble than any one boy or man should ever have.

"A spade is a spade with you, as always," Algernon said on a long suffering sigh. "Yes, I admit that I did find the idea of such a connection to be very appealing. I didn't tell Olivia because I knew that she would have said yes. She had adored you for years, had all but worshipped you when she was a girl. So, yes, my vanity is solely responsible for every horrific event that has unfolded since--the end of our friendship, the fact that Olivia was not happily married to you when Melville discovered the extent of her inheritance and decided to claim it for himself."

He stopped, drew a deep breath, and did the one thing that Burke had never known Algernon to do in all of their long acquaintance. He apologized. "I'm sorry. For the pain I have caused you both. If I had agreed to allow you to court Olivia, the two of you would be wed now, I would have a niece or nephew to dandle on my knee, and Olivia's reputation would not be in tatters. It is all, completely and entirely, my fault."

Burke still wanted to pound his fist into Algernon's face, though the urge was fading. He wasn't precisely sympathetic, but the very sincere contrition made it difficult to cling to anger. "So, what now? We call pax and I should forgive your insults, your lies, your machinations?"

"Not at all. I don't seek forgiveness. There is none

to be had for what I have done. But there is restitution," Algernon stated firmly. "Olivia will not marry you if you ask her outright. She will take it for pity, as she is just as proud as I am. Also, she would suspect that I had spoken with you and would adamantly refuse you... Assuming you still wish to wed Olivia? Or did I misinterpret the depth of your feelings for her?"

Burke drained the snifter of brandy, not even tasting the heady liquid. He let it burn a trail, hot and potent, to his gut, before promptly refilling the glass. "My feelings for Olivia have not changed, have never changed. But they are between Olivia and myself, and I will not discuss them with you again."

Algernon nodded, "Of course not. So, if you wish to wed Olivia, then you will have to convince her and there is nothing more effective at clouding a woman's judgment and making her question her own decisions than seduction. I think that if you want her, you will have to first accept her on her terms."

Burke expelled a heavy sigh, "I cannot believe you are urging me to seduce your own bloody sister."

Algernon shrugged. "We have adapted to our change in social circumstance. The proper way, in this instance, is not the right way."

"I will consider it."

Algernon nodded and rose from the table. Rather than walking away immediately, he hesitated. Looking back, he said, "For what it's worth, I truly am sorry... Also, I should tell you that Olivia's memory of those events is somewhat lacking. She does not remember that you rescued her and that bit of grist thankfully never made it into the gossip mill."

It was only a few moments later that Burke's lunch was delivered to his table. It sat before him, untouched, as he wrestled with the devil's bargain that had just been placed before him. He had been offered a chance to have the one thing he had desired most in his life, but in doing so, he would have to compromise every scruple he possessed.

He would do it, of course. Any chance to have Olivia in his life again would be worth whatever price he had to pay. But if it *didn't* work, if as her lover, he could not convince her to be his wife, what then? Walking away from her before had been its own sort of hell. What would it be like if he had to walk away after having her?

***

At a nearby table, Richard Farnsworth, Lord Hurston, watched the exchange with a keen eye. For Dunne and Holland to be communicating, there could only be one reason. Miss Olivia Dunne.

He cursed beneath his breath. Whatever the two were colluding on would necessitate moving up his plans.

A dark shadow fell across the table and he looked up to see the glowering countenance of Lord Wilmont. "You've been curiously absent from your home, Hurston."

Hurston offered a grim smile. "My home is quite overrun with debt collectors of late… of which you are one."

"I am losing my patience with you, Hurston. You have a fortnight to repay your markers or I shall see you ruined. Are we clear?"

"I have the means to repay you close at hand, Wilmont."

Lord Wilmont's gaze traveled across the club to the retreating back of Algernon Dunne. "If you intend to utilize the same means Melville had his eyes on, I'd caution you to recall how poorly that ended for him."

Hurston glared up at him. "I've a firmer hand than Melville. She'll not get away from me."

"We are all aware of your firm hand, Hurston. It's why you've been banned from half the brothels in London. Just get the funds, Hurston, and be done with it."

Chapter Three

Olivia had dressed for the Somerfield ball with greater care than she could ever recall. The dress she had chosen was ivory satin. The sleeves and hem were embroidered in gold with a Greek key design. A daring décolletage displayed her abundant bosom to great effect. Beneath the gown, she wore only one petticoat, allowing the shimmering satin to cling to her body with every move.

It was daring. In fact, she had nearly balked when the carriage had halted in front of Somerfield House. It had been Algernon's presence in the carriage that had prompted her to disembark and meet her fate, as it were. His challenging stare had steeled her determination to forge ahead in spite of her attack of nerves.

As she made the rounds of the crowded ballroom, she ignored the scandalized stares leveled at her by the society matrons. A few gentlemen asked her to dance, though her dance card was far from full. She refused to consider how much that had changed since she'd attended the Somerfield ball the year before.

The evening was wearing on and she had yet to see any sign of Burke. Algernon had assured her that he would be present. She had no idea how he had come by that bit of information, but she imagined that it involved flirtation or bribery. She begged off a dance with Lord Halcomb, who in his exuberance had stepped on her hem. It wasn't surprising given that he had been so intently focused on her bosom he'd been all but tripping over his own feet. Disheartened, she retreated to the ladies' withdrawing room to repair the damage.

Ducking behind one of the many chinoiserie screens that had been placed about the room, she allowed one of the maids to assist her in repairing the ravaged hem. The maid clucked her tongue disapprovingly as she placed small, perfect stitches along the line of delicate embroidery. The outer door opened and the low hum of feminine voices became more audible.

"Did you see her flirting with him so *shamelessly*?"

A low titter followed the comment, and the voice that replied was horrifyingly familiar. "She's *positively* shameless... It isn't as if anyone here doesn't know about her affair with Melville!"

Lady Caroline Bishop had been Olivia's rival in admiration and popularity in former seasons. No one had reveled in Olivia's fall quite so much as Caroline. Even now, a year later, she was still trotting out the tired old gossip. Olivia placed her finger to her lips, gesturing for silence, before the maid could speak. The bobbing of her white cap was the only reply.

The first woman continued, "That gown is *scandalous!* But what else could be expected of her?"

A third woman entered the room, "Quickly, you must come! Lord Holland has arrived." The voice had belonged to Lady Caroline's mother. It galled Olivia that the other woman had set her sights on Burke.

When the three women had left hurriedly, she gestured to the maid, "It doesn't have to be perfect, just quick."

"All finished, miss," the maid said, "And I know it isn't my place, but you're a finer lady than the likes of them witches could ever be."

Olivia laughed, "I won't repeat it, and I do appreciate it very much." She was still chuckling softly to herself as she returned to the ballroom. Algernon greeted her immediately.

"The object of your campaign stepped out onto the terrace. I imagine now would be an appropriate time for you to take some air."

Olivia watched her brother walk away and wondered at how surprisingly helpful he was being in guiding her along the path to ruination. She didn't doubt for one moment that he had an ulterior motive; one that was, without doubt, in what he considered to be her best interests. Regardless, it did not sway her from her plan.

She turned toward the open doors of the terrace. There were many people strolling about the terrace, looking out onto the moonlit garden. It wasn't simply the romantic atmosphere that the scene provided, however. Lady Somerfield was mad to have her every ball named The Crush of the Season. She invited far more people than her ballroom would accommodate and the result was always stifling heat that sent many of the ladies present into delicate swoons. The one benefit to the mad crowd was that it was fairly easy to disappear among the throng.

She spotted Burke instantly. He stood alone, leaning against the railing, in full view of the ballroom. Rather than looking out at the garden, he was facing the doors, gazing in at the dancers. It was an apt image. Burke had been the object of many scandals, most of them created by his family, but the burden of them had fallen onto his shoulders. Like her, he was on the outside of society looking in. She approached him casually, trying to disguise both her eagerness and her nerves.

He was, if possible, even more handsome than he had been when last she had seen him. His hair was thick and dark, combed back from his face in disregard of the current fashion of artfully tousled waves and curls. The idea of Burke submitting to a valet armed with curling tongs was preposterous. The slight widow's peak made him appear dangerous, as did the dark slashes of brows above his pale green eyes.

At two and thirty, his face had lost all hint of boyishness, leaving behind stark planes and angles that were the very definition of masculine beauty. His shoulders appeared to be broader than they'd been in his youth, making his waist and hips appear lean. His long legs were stretched out in front of him, his feet crossed at the ankles as he reclined against the railing. The casual stance did nothing to hide the heavy musculature of his thighs.

She knew the minute that he saw her, could feel his gaze upon her. She looked up and met his eyes, thankful for the dim light which would conceal her blush at having been caught perusing his masculine charms. A cool smile curved his lips as he rose to his full height and sketched a bow to her.

"Good evening, Miss Dunne. Availing yourself of the fresh air that is in such short supply within?"

"Indeed, Lord Holland. I found the heat to be quite stifling. You are looking well."

"And you are a vision, as always," he replied. It was true. Olivia was always beautiful, always alluring, but in such a daring gown, with the upper swells of her breasts entirely bare, and the fabric clinging to her legs as she strode forward, it had had never been more true. Her glorious hair was piled atop her head in an artful arrangement of curls. It gave one the impression that the slightest breeze would send the mass of curls tumbling down her back in wanton disarray. It would not, of course, but the effect was nonetheless provocative.

"You were always a flatterer. It has been far too long since we have spoken," she said, her voice slightly chiding.

He nodded his agreement. "I must beg your forgiveness for my lack of attentiveness. I am a poor friend, in deed."

"Are we friends, then?"

He considered his answer carefully. Saying too much or saying too little could tip the balance in a way he did not wish. "We are of a long acquaintance. I have always enjoyed your company, and I would only ever wish the best of things for you. If that is not friendship, what is?"

"Is there not a certain amount of intimacy in true friendship?" she inquired boldly.

He could feel his body responding to that coy question. The blood rushed in his veins and his body stirred uncomfortably. Did she fully understand everything that she implied with her words? Or was his foreknowledge of her purpose coloring his interpretation? "I suppose that is true... What sort of intimacy do you require in friendship, Olivia?"

She took a deep breath, releasing it on a sigh. He could see her gathering her courage. A part of him wished to spare her that, but it was her game, and he would have to play accordingly.

"That would depend entirely upon the friend... I think perhaps this is something we should discuss more privately?"

It was not the most provocative proposition he'd ever received, but by far the most tempting. Though they were in full view of the ballroom, Olivia had her back to the doors. She was standing slightly in front of him, so that he was partially concealed from view. He lifted his hand and placed it atop hers on the railing. He drew circles on the delicate skin at the inside of her wrist with his thumb and she shivered slightly in response. "There is a small parlor just down the hall from the ladies' withdrawing room. Ten minutes," he said, withdrawing his hand from hers.

***

Burke used the short reprieve in the small parlor to collect his thoughts and to attempt to gain control over his wayward libido. Before he'd pressed his summarily rejected suit, he'd never dared stand so close to Olivia. Given his reputation and hers, he'd always been the soul of propriety with her. Accessing every shred of his willpower, he tamped down the desire that coursed through his veins. He had no intention of taking Olivia in a drawing room only a few doors from a crowded ballroom.

He'd avoided her for the past year, in part because of Algernon's dismissal of his suit and their subsequent falling out, but also because he hadn't wished to remind her of such painful events. Recalling Algernon's statement that her memories of the rescue were incomplete and unreliable, he realized that his avoidance had all been for naught.

The sound of the door opening pulled him from his thoughts. He looked up to see Olivia walk in and she literally took his breath away. It wasn't simply that she was beautiful. Though remarkably so, he'd known other women who were as beautiful, if not more so. It was simply that she was *Olivia*.

Her dress swayed with each step as she entered the room, and with the moonlight filtering through the windows, she glowed. "I had wondered if you would lose your nerve," he said. Her answering smile curved gently over her lips and once again, set his blood pounding.

"Have you ever known me to lose my nerve?"

"This is rather scandalous behavior, Miss Dunne— meeting a gentleman in a darkened room at a ball. But you did request privacy, did you not?" he asked, keeping his tone light and teasing. Flirtation. Seduction. The slow build of desire. Those were the things that she required. Not the intense, stabbing need that battered him in her presence.

"It might have escaped your notice, Lord Holland, but I am now a scandalous woman," Olivia said. She moved deeper into the room, coming to stand before the windows. Her words were bold, but as he stepped closer to her, he heard the slight catch of her breath. He could feel the tension in her as she attempted to brazen it out.

Burke inhaled, breathing in the light, floral scent that clung to her hair. There was a slight hint of citrus, as well. He knew that she used lemons on her skin, despising even a hint of freckles. She'd wept over the smattering of freckles on her nose as a child, when others had teased her, but he found them charming, as always. "Hardly scandalous. I have known you for the better part of your life and can count on one hand, actually one finger, the number of times you've behaved improperly…including this meeting. I count myself a fortunate man indeed to be the one you have chosen as cohort as you dip your toes into the scandal broth. But perhaps you should tell me why?"

"Why what?" she asked, her mouth suddenly dry.

"There are many options. Why did you seek me out tonight when we haven't spoken in years? Why did you agree to meet with me privately when you know it's improper? Why did you don a dress that is infinitely more revealing than anything you have ever worn, while wearing only one petticoat beneath it?"

She glanced back at him, "How do you know how many petticoats I have on?"

He smiled, "You question my knowledge of my feminine undergarments?"

Chuckling, she replied, "Of course. What was I thinking?"

His reply was closer to her ear; a hot, seductive whisper. "Precisely. What were you thinking, Olivia?"

Shivering in response, Olivia turned to face him. Standing as close as he was, her breasts were a breath away from touching his chest. Leaning forward as he was, they were nose to nose. "I was thinking that we should renew our acquaintance."

He raised his eyebrow, and when he spoke, his breath fanned across her cheek. "That necessitated our meeting outside the ballroom, away from any prying eyes?"

He was forcing her to be bold, forcing her to state unequivocally what she wanted from him. Burke would flirt with her, but he would proceed no further unless she stated very specifically that she wished for him to do so. "As I said, I was hoping that our friendship might become more intimate… much more intimate."

He kissed her cheek. It was something he'd done

many times over the years, but it was not the brotherly peck she'd received as a child. It was slower, potent, and conveyed infinitely more than just affection. "Is that intimate enough for you, Olivia?" he whispered against her ear.

"Is that how a notorious rake steals a kiss, then? On the cheek?"

"I'm reformed," he replied. "Or had you not noticed that I'd escaped your brother's damning influence?"

Her nose wrinkled in distaste. "I did not allow you to lure me into a darkened room to discuss my brother!"

Burke raised an eyebrow at that. "I'm quite sure you did the luring... I merely provided the location. And if you've no wish to discuss your brother, Olivia, what burning topic is on your mind?"

She trembled slightly, but pressed on, "I had wanted to make you an offer, one I hope you cannot refuse."

"Do go on."

When she spoke again, her voice was soft, little more than a whisper. It reflected her uncertainty, her inexperience, but it was still potent, calling to every carnal instinct he possessed.

"I've decided to take a lover… and I'd very much like it to be you."

Even expecting it, the words were like a punch to the gut. His blood pooled low in his belly, racing to his hardening cock.

Still, his response was measured and slow as his lips moved over the curve of her cheek, to press lightly against the corner of her mouth, before settling more firmly over her lips. They were soft and full beneath him, sweetly yielding as he explored.

When she sighed, his lips curved in a smile, but he pressed on, wanting more. He traced the lush curve of her lower lip with his tongue, nipped it gently with his teeth, and then lightly traced the seam of her lips. Her lips parted on another sigh and he seized the opportunity to invade the sweet recesses of her mouth. His tongue glided sensuously over hers. Each touch was soft, gentle and infused with languorous heat.

Olivia was spiraling into nothingness. Her mind had long since ceased to function and every sense had become attuned to the kiss, the erotic and seductive movement of his mouth over hers. Breathless, her knees weak, she pressed her hands against his chest for balance. The heat of him, the firm muscles that flexed beneath her touch only unnerved her more.

She felt his arms wrap around her, pulling her closer to him. With only the thin silk of her gown and the single petticoat, she could feel the hard press of his thighs against hers and against the soft curve of her belly, something else. Her knowledge was not so limited that she didn't recognize his arousal for what it was, but she couldn't allow herself to think about it. Panic would follow and that would lead to something disastrous like running away from what she wanted simply because it was unknown.

Burke had never known anything as glorious as the feel of her in his arms. The sweetness of her mouth, the warmth of her lush curves against him, the way her flesh yielded to his, all combined to have him aching and desperate for her. It was that edge of desperation that prompted him to pull back. He didn't quite trust himself.

"Olivia," he said, and his voice was ragged with need, "This is not the place."

"You started it," she said, her voice husky and breathless.

He laughed. Though he was in a misery of desire, the tight evening breeches like a vise over his aching shaft, he couldn't deny the truth of her statement. "You're absolutely right. A more important question would be whether or not you wish me to finish it."

A blush stole over her cheeks, deepening their already rosy hue. "Would I be here otherwise?"

Now, he thought. He wanted nothing more than to strip the gown from her and memorize every curve, every valley before sinking into the welcoming heat of her body. Awakening Olivia to passion was something he had fantasized about for years. "Are you engaged for tomorrow night?"

An arch look crossed her face, eyebrows arcing upward and her lips forming a thin line. "My social calendar is rather sparse these days."

It would be. Society loved nothing better than to watch their icons fall. "I'll send my carriage for you at midnight… assuming that your brother will not be home."

"Algernon and I have reached an understanding about my choices. He doesn't like it, but he won't interfere."

He hadn't thought she'd be so forthcoming with that information. "Why have you chosen me, Olivia?" The question had sprung unbidden to his lips. Immediately, he regretted asking.

Her lips parted as she considered her answer carefully. "Because you're beautiful."

"Men are not beautiful," he reproofed with a smile. "We are handsome. But never beautiful."

But he was. Not simply physically, though Burke was certainly one of the most handsome men she'd ever seen. There was a kindness in him that few would note, primarily because she doubted he showed that to many others. But she'd seen it first hand. Not once since her disgrace had his treatment of her changed. Yes, he was distant, but he had been before thanks to his falling out with Algernon. She still wondered at that, at why they had simply stopped speaking to one another. She continued, ignoring his correction, "And for whatever reason that your friendship with

Algernon disintegrated, you haven't treated me differently. Yes, you were distant, but you were distant before my reputation was in tatters. You've treated me no differently since…and I trust you."

"To be discreet?"

She nodded, "To be discreet. To be the wonderful lover that you are rumored to be. And, to protect me from any unforeseen consequences, as I lack the knowledge and experience to do so."

The very idea of Olivia carrying his child was so seductively appealing to him. Could he do that to her, take the trust she was placing in him and intentionally misuse it? No. He would protect her, though it was contrary to the very thing he wanted. Still, he warned her, "I will do what I can, Olivia, but you must understand that even the most effective methods do fail. If that happens—"

She stopped him with a kiss. It lacked expertise but was achingly sweet for it. "We will deal with it if or when we must. In the meantime, can't we just enjoy it, enjoy each other?"

Her untutored kiss was achingly sweet and more

tempting than the most skilled courtesan. "Tomorrow night, Olivia... Be certain this is what you want. Be absolutely certain."

For the past year, uncertainty had dogged her every step. It was gone now. There wasn't a doubt in her mind that she wanted Burke. "I am certain. Absolutely certain."

***

Returning from the ball, the interior of the carriage was quiet. But Olivia felt Algernon's regard. "If you've something to say, brother, please do so. Your silence grows tiresome."

Algernon was silent for a moment longer, then spoke solemnly. "Has he agreed to your terms, then?"

"He has," Olivia replied softly. "You won't interfere, Algie. You promise?"

He held up his hands in supplication. "My interference in this affair, pardon the unfortunate word choice, is at an end. You've made your decision and apparently so has Burke."

Curiosity sparked in her. "What happened to end your friendship?"

"I was a pompous, preening ass, of course, and Burke lost patience with me, as it were," he offered vaguely.

"I still plan to move to the house on Brooke Street," she said softly. "And it isn't simply because of my arrangement with Burke. I meant it when I said that you should have a wife, Algie. And I am an impediment to that."

"Let us not jump too far ahead, Liv," he said. "We'll see what happens with Burke and then we'll decide later. I've no wish to rattle around in that house alone."

The carriage rolled to a stop and the steps were lowered by a waiting footman. Algernon alighted and then helped her down.

Olivia saw no reason to be insistent based on his response, not without seeming a spoiled brat. So, she acquiesced at least momentarily, and allowed him to escort her into the house. She was eager for her bed, eager for the reprieve of sleep from the nerves that had plagued her through the day.

***

In the shadowy mews behind the row of Mayfair townhouses, the men watched. "Why are we 'ere?" the first one asked, scratching at his head.

"To get paid, you lump," the second one replied. "'E wants to know what she's about and we need to keep'im informed!"

"She's about boring us into an early grave, is all she's about," the first man snapped. "I always thought these toffs 'ad it made, but if I lived like'er, I'd be taking a dip in the Thames and not coming back up!"

A rusty chuckle escaped his companion. "Right enough. I'm done for. She's in for the night and'e'll be wantin' a report." If'n she'd ever go somewhere without that brother of'ers, we'd be out of this mess."

"Let's go, Charlie… 'Fore someone sees us and calls the watch."

Chapter Four

The following night, Burke was in his library, waiting. The servants had been dismissed for the evening, except for his butler, whom he trusted to be discreet. His heart
was pounding and he was so nervous, one would have
thought he was the virgin.

A light meal had been laid out for them before the
fire, along with champagne. Olivia had expressed an affini-
ty for it to him at one point, and he knew the bubbling liquid would ease what nerves she might have. He had no intention of allowing her to get too deeply into her cups, but a
bit of relaxation would hardly be amiss.

His pulse leapt when he heard the door open and
shut. The light tread of her slippers on the floor was torture.
It seemed to take an eternity for her to reach the library.

He opened before she could even knock. She stood
before him in a heavy cloak, the hood drawn up to conceal
her face. Even then, he would have known it was her. He
could smell the same floral and citrus scent that had driven
him mad the night before. He'd been able to smell it on his

clothes after their kiss and it had haunted him. "Come in," he said, and even to his own ears, he sounded desperate. Striving for an appearance of, if not neutrality, then at least a normal level of anticipation, he stepped back from the door so she could enter. He watched her walking across the room to the small table laid before the hearth. Even the way she moved was unconsciously seductive. The graceful, feminine sway of her hips was hypnotic.

Olivia heard the door shut, and knew that they were alone. Pushing back the hood of her cloak, she turned to face him. He wore only breeches and a simple shirt. His cravat and waistcoat were long since discarded, and his hair was deliciously tousled, as if he'd just run his hands through it. "This is very romantic. I didn't imagine you would stage a seduction when we've already reached an agreement."

Burke smiled, "Seduction isn't simply to secure consent. It can be a pleasure in and of itself."

She smiled at the sentiment. "Are you a romantic, then?"

He chuckled, as he opened the champagne. "I am a

man. But for Byron and those other puppies that moon over young ladies at balls, none of us like to be called such a thing. No, I prefer to think that I am a man who understands what a woman desires."

Olivia shivered, as much from his tone as his words. His voice held the promise of pleasure. Remembering the desire that he had stoked in her the night before with no more than a kiss, she trembled slightly as she moved to unfasten her cloak. He placed the champagne bottle on the table and moved to assist her. His hands did little more than brush her shoulders, and still it left her weak. "Then it appears I have chosen well," she said, attempting to sound blasé.

Burke might have been offended by her words, as if he were nothing more than stud to service her, but there was a faint tremor in her voice, a vulnerability that revealed far more than she would have wished. Draping the cloak across the back of one of the chairs, he took in her appearance. She wore a simple gown, one that would be easy enough to get into and out of without the benefit of a maid. Likewise her hair had been dressed simply. It was tied back from her face with a ribbon, making her look younger, and for one brief moment he regretted what was about to come. But he reminded himself that it was the only way. His intentions for her were honorable, even if her own were not.

The light from the hearth glinted on her hair, making it gleam. "You are so lovely," he said simply.

"For the longest time, I wondered if you even recognized that I was a woman," she said with a hint of amusement. "I thought perhaps to you I was simply some sort of sexless creature, tolerated only because I was Algernon's sister."

"Never that," he said. "I was always aware of you as a woman. Too aware—from the time you were sixteen and came to dinner in your first evening gown. You wore your hair up that night, and I wondered that your slender neck could even support the weight."

Olivia's lips parted in surprise. She'd never known, never realized that he saw her. "You hid it well."

He'd had to. At that point he'd been on the verge of losing everything that wasn't entailed and had been hanging onto the last shred of his family's respectability by a thread. Any hint at that time that his feelings for her had been anything other than brotherly and Algernon would have called him out, with good reason. "You were very young. Anything else would have been dishonorable," he said simply. It was not entirely true, but it was close enough.

Olivia accepted the proffered glass of champagne, sipping until the bubbles burned her nose. Heat of a different kind spread through her belly, and some of the tension that had tormented her through the day eased. She tossed back the remainder of the liquid, and held her glass out for a refill. His raised eyebrow was his only outward response. She noted that when he refilled her glass, it was with a more moderate amount.

"It would hardly do to have you so foxed you lapse into unconsciousness," he said.

Her nerves, in spite of his efforts, were getting the better of her. The fear of the unknown loomed, growing ever more distressing with each passing moment. To that end, she spoke, "I do appreciate this, Burke. It was very sweet of you to set such a lush and charming scene, as you said. But if it isn't too much trouble, I'd prefer if we could simply—"

"If you say you wish to be done with it, my ego may never recover."

"It isn't that… Well it *is*, but not because I do not want to do this. It's just that the longer we wait, the more nervous I become and if we wait much longer, I may lose my nerve entirely. So, if we could actually just… get on with it?" What had begun as a halting explanation ended with her words tripping over one another in her haste to get them out.

"Then by all means follow me," he said, and led her from the library, up the stairs and toward his chambers. The door had no sooner closed behind them than he had tugged her into his arms and claimed her lips.

His kiss was more intoxicating than champagne. As his lips molded to hers and his tongue stole boldly into her mouth, she was shocked at the carnality of it.

Heat swept through her until her breasts ached and she had to tamp down the urge to squeeze her thighs together to relieve the ache that had settled low in her belly.

She could feel the dampness forming at the juncture of her thighs. Not entirely ignorant of what was to happen, she marveled that he had managed to elicit such a response with nothing more than a kiss.

Burke loosened the ribbon from her hair, threading his fingers through the silken strands as he left the honeyed sweetness of her mouth to trail hot, wet kisses over the column of her throat. His hands moved from her hair, down her back, over her ribs, until his thumbs rested at the undersides of her lush breasts.

"I never imagined seduction would feel like this," she said breathlessly.

"And how does it feel?"

"Unbearably hot, as if my very blood is set to boil. My clothes feel too tight on my skin, and yet, as warm as I am, I cannot help but want to be even closer to you," she confessed.

"That, my dear," he replied, closing one hand fully over her breast, his thumb stroking over the hardened bud of her nipple, "Is precisely what seduction feels like."

"Touch me then, Burke," she whispered, "Make me

burn."

He needed no further urging. Tugging at the bodice of her dress, he pulled it down until he could see the dark circles of her nipples peeking above the edge of her chemise and stays. He closed his hands over her breasts, kneading the soft mounds gently, the tips of his fingers moving over the distended buds of her nipples. He hadn't expected that she would be so passionate, so eager but it thrilled him.

With his hands at her breasts, and his teeth scraping gently over the tender skin of her throat, she moaned. It was an earthy sound, and it tested his resolve to be gentle. Reluctantly, he moved his hands away from the lush bounty long enough to loosen the ties of her gown. When it gaped slightly he reached for the tapes of her stays, loosening them as well, until the slipped free entirely.

Her breasts were full; their dusky, pink tips hard and swollen. He bent his head, pressing soft kisses along the swells of her breasts, until he reached a pebbled peak. His pressed his tongue against her, circling that tight bud, before flicking gently. Encouraged by her soft moans and the arch of her back which had thrust her breasts forward for his greedy hands and mouth, he closed his lips over her nipple, suckling deeply.

"Burke!" she gasped, shocked by the maelstrom of sensations swirling inside her. She had asked him to make her burn, but in truth, she hadn't known what that meant, in truth. The gentle heat that had assailed her before had sparked into a raging inferno within her.

"You wanted passion, Olivia," he said. "You wanted to burn."

"More," she urged, "I want more."

Quickly, he stripped off her gown, shoving the fabric down until it bunched at her waist, before tugging the skirt up until it bared the silken skin of her thighs. There were no petticoats beneath the gown, only her chemise, silk so fine it was all but transparent.

Below the hem of the chemise, which stopped at the tops of her creamy thighs, he could see her embroidered garters and silk stockings. He had never seen anything as perfect as she was. Her lush full breasts tapered to a small waist just above the flare of her hip made his mouth go dry.

He could all but feel her silk clad thighs wrapping around him. The thought increased the ache of his already rigid cock.

Burke scooped her into his arms and carried her to the bed. Rather than joining her immediately, he stepped back, his eyes traveling over her from the loose, fiery waves of her hair down her silk clad body to her slippered feet.

Under his gaze, Olivia felt both intense desire and intense embarrassment. She had never been displayed such. The desire to cover her breasts, to conceal the darker curls at the juncture of her thighs warred with the thrill she felt at the hot look in his eyes. It was what she had always wanted, she realized, to have Burke looking at her with desire, to see her as a woman rather than as his friend's younger sister. Given his obvious appreciation for her figure now, she was left with little doubt as to his vision of her as a woman grown.

"I don't know what to do," she confessed. "I understand what is to happen… in theory, but the reality of it escapes me."

His answering smile accompanied his strong hand encircling her ankle. Lifting her foot, he traced his thumbs over the fine bones, before removing the embroidered slipper. "First, you have to relax."

With his hands kneading the tension from her body, his skilled fingers sliding over her silk clad foot, her ankle, and then gliding along the curve of her calf, she wasn't simply relaxed, she was melting. "I thought there would be slightly greater participation required on my part."

"We'll get to that," he murmured, as his hands continued their exploration, gliding sensuously over her thigh, to the neatly tied bow that held her garter in place. A single tug and it gave way, and with a practiced motion, he rolled the silk stocking down her leg, the callused pads of his fingers moving sensuously over her satiny skin. When he had finished, and the garment slid over her delicately arched foot, he pressed a kiss into the arch, causing her to shiver. The process was repeated until she was left wearing only her chemise. When he reached for it, she stopped him, placing her hands over his.

"Have you changed your mind, then?" he asked. He

would let her go. It might kill him, but he would do it.

She smiled, a slight turning of her lips that set his heart to thumping. "No, but it isn't fair that I'm all but naked, and you are still fully clothed."

Automatically, he reached for his shirt and pulled it over his head and tossed it to the floor. "Is that enough for now?"

At the sight of his chest, Olivia simply couldn't breathe. Hard, sculpted muscles flexed and rippled beneath bronzed skin. The light dusting of hair intrigued her; it spread over his chest before narrowing to a thin line that arrowed down into the waistband of his breeches. Tentatively, she reached out, her fingertips brushing across his skin, eliciting a groan from him. The texture of his skin, the heat that poured from him, and the brush of crisp hair were so alien to her and yet so incredibly enticing. "I know you said men are not supposed to be beautiful, but you are."

Burke captured her hand, pulling it to his mouth, and kissing her palm, before pushing her back onto the bed. Not wanting to crush her, he rested his weight on his elbow while he kissed her cheek, her neck, the delicate line of her collarbone. He dipped his tongue into the hollow of her throat and then trailed hot, wet kisses down to the soft mounds of her breasts. "Can we dispose of this now?" he asked, tugging at the hem of her chemise. She blushed but nodded her consent.

He dispensed with it quickly and it joined the other items that already littered the floor. The thatch of auburn curls at the apex of her thighs beckoned to him. His hand coasted across her hip, over her belly, to brush those tight curls. She gasped, but made no protest. With soft teasing strokes, he moved over the mound of her sex. Gradually, she relaxed. He could feel the tension recede from her, and then his hand dipped lower, the tips of his fingers touching the damp cleft, before slipping inside her. With a shudder, she opened to him, her thighs parting to his questing hand. Deepening the strokes, he touched the most sensitive parts of her, and she moaned. That rich, earthy sound spiked his own need to all new levels.

"Burke," she said, his name escaping as half sigh, half cry. "That feels so good."

He kissed her, "There's more…so much more."

With his hand buried between her thighs, and his mouth again at her breasts, Olivia couldn't imagine that anything could feel more wonderful. But as his mouth skated over her skin, moving down from her breasts, over her belly, she began to panic. Before she could even give voice to the protest that had blossomed in her mind, his mouth was *there*. She could no longer think, or reason, only *feel*.

Burke tasted her, tracing his tongue over the slick, honeyed folds of her sex. He flicked his tongue over the hardened bud of her clitoris and reveled in her answering moan. Continuing the exquisite torment, he took note of her response. The tension in her thighs, the slight quiver of her belly told him that she was so close to her release. He slid his finger inside her, marveling at how tight she was, while he continued driving her upwards with his lips and tongue. She writhed beneath him, but he placed one hand firmly over her belly, holding her to him.

Each soft cry from her parted lips, each shudder beneath his mouth was a victory for him, but when he felt her pulsing beneath him, the rippling of her sheath around his fingers as her first climax took her he was awed and eager.

He wanted to be inside her, to feel the liquid heat of her body surrounding him, welcoming him.

Olivia felt him move between her thighs, felt his hands parting her more fully. The brush of his hair roughened legs against the sensitive skin of her inner thighs only heightened the pleasure that still coursed through her. "Now, Burke... I want you now."

"There's no going back, Olivia... This is your last chance to leave with your virginity intact."

Wrapping her legs more tightly around him, she said, "Are you trying to talk me out of it?"

On a groan, he said, "No, but I would hate for you to have regrets."

Arching against him, loving the feel of his hard body between her thighs, the weight of him on top of her, she sighed, "My only regret is waiting so long."

Burke hissed a breath between clenched teeth. For a virgin, she was damnably bold. The combination of innocence and carnality was driving him wild. Reaching between their bodies, he parted her and guided only the tip of his shaft inside. The heat was scalding and the hot clutch of her feminine flesh around him was all that he had dreamed of. He pressed forward, thrusting deeper inside her until he reached the barrier of her innocence. Claiming her mouth, he swallowed her sharp cry with his mouth as he thrust fully inside her.

Forcing himself to remain perfectly still as he waited for the pain to subside, he kissed her cheek, her neck, and against the soft shell of her ear, whispered a fervent apology. "I'm so sorry, Olivia. It will ease in a moment."

It was already easing. The pain had been fleeting, but the alien sensation of having him inside her was still taking some getting used to. It wasn't quite what she had imagined. "It's fine," she said. "It doesn't hurt anymore."

Burke looked down at her, at the delicate bone structure and porcelain perfect skin, now flushed with passion. "It gets better," he said with a small smile, and then moved, gently flexing his hips.

That small movement changed everything. The pleasure returned as swiftly as it had fled. "Oh. I can certainly see that it does," she murmured breathlessly.

He would have smiled, enjoying her banter, but his

attention was focused intently on the task at hand. Specifically, not going off like an untried boy. Surging more deeply inside her, feeling her heated flesh closing around him, he struggled for some semblance of control. Setting an easy rhythm, he watched her every response, taking in every soft sigh, every ragged breath, the way her eyes fluttered closed and her head fell back against the pillows.

Her breath rushed out on a sharp cry and her nails scored his back as she arched beneath him. The quivering of her belly and the tension in her thighs intensified. Knowing that she was hovering on the precipice of release spiked his own need. Hooking one hand behind her knee, he hitched her leg higher on his hip, altering the angle ever so slightly.

Her indrawn breath was held, her body drawing taut beneath him as her sheath clamped around him, drawing him deeper, holding onto him. Every spasm battered his control. Desperate, he thrust one last time and then withdrew, spilling himself on her thigh rather than in the welcoming haven of her body.

Holding himself above her, his breathing ragged

and sweat slicking his skin, Burke had just committed possibly the greatest sin of his life. He only wished he were an honorable enough man to regret it.

CHAPTER FIVE

"Why are you here?"

Charlie and Martin looked at one another nervously. "She's gone out for the night. All night. To a fancy 'ouse on Curzon Street."

Neither of them was prepared for the response of their employer. The heavy crystal glass in his hand shattered against the door directly behind them. "Alone… at night? Unescorted?"

Charlie nodded. "Aye, m'lord."

The toff, as they referred to him, glared at them. "I've paid you to watch her, to observe her, and when the opportunity presented itself *to nab her*. And she went out in the dark, alone, and you failed, miserably, you worthless bastards."

Neither man took offense at being called a bastard. For both of them, it was simply the truth of their circumstances of birth. "There weren't much opportunity. She walked out of the'ouse covered in a big'eavy cloak, climbed into the carriage waitin' there, and off she went. We followed behind, cuttin' through the mews and found'er just as she was goin' into the other'ouse," Martin answered.

"This carriage… did it have any identifying marks?"

"No, m'lord. But them'orses would be easy to spot. Big'uns. Coal black, long, curling manes. Prettiest beasts I've ever seen."

The man smiled then. "Gentleman, you just earned your pay… Keep watching her. Do nothing more than monitor her activities until you hear otherwise from me. If she's formed an attachment with the gentleman I suspect, I may very well be able to use that to bring her to heel without resorting to violence."

"I don't understand," Charlie said.

The toff looked at them then, with his cold, dead eyes. "I don't pay you to understand. Just report to me the next time she goes to that house. Immediately."

The men nodded and left quickly. Once outside, Martin looked at Charlie. "I don't care what 'e's paying us. I wish we'd never took this job."

Charlie nodded. "But we did. And I don't think 'e's

the type to just let us quit. 'E'd stab us as soon as look at us."

"What do you think'e'll do to'er then?"

Charlie shrugged. "Better'er than us."

***

Olivia awoke to the soft brush of lips against the nape of her neck, just below the sweep of her hair. She smiled. Her smile faded into a wince as she stretched and felt the tender protests of muscles in response to her exertions of the previous evening.

"Sore?" Burke whispered against her ear. "How on earth did that happen?"

She blushed. "You know very well how it happened. I've behaved scandalously enough without indulging in such scandalous conversation!"

He chuckled softly. "You said many scandalous things last night, Olivia. And soon, you'll be saying many more."

Her heart thundered at the sensual promise in his tone. "How soon?"

"Not tonight. I fear I'm old and you've worn me

out," he teased.

She rolled over on her back and glared at him. It was still dark outside, but at some point, he'd gotten up to stoke the fire. With the light from it, she could see him clearly as he lay above the covers. Naked. His hair disheveled from her own restless hands. The dark shadow of whiskers enhanced the planes of his face. He was so handsome it took her breath away. And he was her lover.

"I never thought to be in such a state with you," she said. "Ever."

His lips firmed with a frown and his brows dipped in a worried scowl. "Do you regret this, Olivia?"

The note of hurt in his voice, of remorse, did not escape her. "Not in the least. How could I? You've given me so much more than I could have hoped for. I had wanted to know passion, to know pleasure… but never in my wildest imaginings could I have envisioned what occurred in this bed with you."

"We need to get you home before the day breaks," he insisted. "Get up and I'll help you to dress."

"So very eager to be shed of me! It isn't like I have

a reputation to protect, Burke," she insisted.

"You do… as do I. I agreed to be your lover, Olivia. I will not be the instrument of your ruin."

"Your instrument is precisely why I am ruined," she said cheekily.

Burke closed his eyes on a groan. "Dear lord. One night of passion and you've become positively debauched and jaded."

"Have I really?" she asked, wide eyed with delight.

He grinned. "Not even close. Last night… was only the beginning. There are so many things, Olivia, that I want you to experience, that I want to teach you. But for now, you must go. Given our enthusiasm last night, and your inexperience, it would be unwise to indulge further."

Rising from the bed and standing before him on legs that trembled, she knew he was right. "Help me. I don't think I can manage on my own."

Burke rose from the bed completely unashamed and lacking even a hint of modesty as he began gathering her clothing. Each layer that he applied to her body was punctuated by kisses and caresses that made her question the need to depart. "Are you certain I must go?"

He stepped closer to her, close enough that she could feel the hard press of him against her hip. There was no longer any question for her of precisely what that meant. Still, he helped her into her chemise and her stays.

"If there were any other way, Olivia, I'd keep you in this bed all day long… but I need to take care of several matters at a small estate I own near Bath. I'll be back in four days time. Sooner if it can be managed."

She didn't want to cling, to need him, but the idea that they would part stung painfully. "I hadn't realized you'd be leaving so soon."

He pulled her against him, her back to his chest and closed his arms about her, pressing a tender kiss against the side of her neck. "It isn't by choice, I promise. I'd much prefer to stay here with you. But this is a matter ignored too long already."

"Upon your return, I'll be residing elsewhere," she said. "I've told Algernon that I wish to take the house on Brooke Street. I've already contacted an agency about hiring a companion to maintain the at least the illusion of respectability."

He grinned at that. "I take it you intend to hire someone with poor eyesight and worse hearing?"

"This is a special kind of agency… After my own fall from grace, I discovered that there is a particular agency that seeks to provide employment for women who have suffered similar fates. It's a very progressive notion," she explained.

"Are you a reformer then?" he asked, placing a tender kiss at her shoulder. It was followed by a soft nip of his teeth that elicited a shiver from her.

"No," she said softly. "I have no wish to take on society. I know only too well how vicious their teeth and claws can be. But I like the idea that I might employ a girl otherwise unemployable and change just her life, if I can."

Burke sighed. She wished to be a savior, to offer someone a respectable future in a way that she felt was lost to her—guilt, regret, a deep and abiding hatred for Melville; all of those things warred inside him. But nothing held such sway over him as his need of her. It burned inside him like a well fed flame.

"Let's get you home before all of London is awake to witness your departure," he said. Retrieving his dressing gown, he donned it quickly and escorted her down the stairs. He paused only long enough to retrieve her cloak from the library. The coachman was waiting out front for her. She had no notion of when he'd had time to arrange that, but she wasn't going to question it. It was quite clear that while he considered himself reformed, he was still quite adept at his rakish ways.

CHAPTER SIX

"Am I to assume you are the inducement luring my sister to a life of independence in a home of her own?"

Burke looked up from his meal to see Algernon striding into the breakfast room as if it were commonplace. His butler, Waldroop, was standing at the door, clearly uncertain of what to do. At one point in time, Dunne striding through the house unannounced was the norm. Waving the elderly man on his way, Burke eyed his uninvited guest.

"Just because I haven't planted my fist in your face, doesn't mean I won't," Burke said dispassionately, then added, "I'm not discussing Olivia with you. Not again."

Algernon was filling a plate at the sideboard. Undoubtedly he'd already eaten in his own dining room but he'd always had a robust appetite. "I misspoke then. It was not a question so much as an observation. The house is in a state. A veritable flurry of activity as she packs up and prepares to move out."

There was a note in Dunne's voice that caused Burke's expression to turn speculative, then harden. "You don't want her to leave… not because you're worried about her, but because you're afraid of being alone."

Algernon seated himself and took a healthy bite of the breakfast he had not been invited to share. He chewed thoughtfully, swallowed and replied, "I have grown accustomed to her presence. But she is correct in her estimation that as long as she remains in residence, I will not marry. Perhaps it is for the best."

The curiosity that piqued in Burke bothered him. He didn't want to care about Algernon or his life or his choice of bride. But he did. "Is there a lady who has sparked your interest, then?"

Algernon grinned. "*Many* have sparked my interest… I have yet to find the one who can retain it."

"I am off to Bath, an estate matter," he explained. "I will see Olivia upon my return… but only Olivia."

Algernon took another bite. "I am not seeking forgiveness. There is none to be had. But in this instance, we should be allies at least. Olivia will confide in me, and what she confides to me may be useful to you in your pursuit of her."

"Until she discovers you are frequenting my home," Burke protested. "At which point she will quickly deduce that there is some scheme afoot. Olivia is not gullible or naive… not any more."

"Or innocent," Algernon shot back. "While I understand the necessity of pursuing her in such an unorthodox fashion—not only that, but at my own suggestion—I still want to murder you for it."

"Olivia is mine. Whether she knows it, accepts it or even agrees to it… she is mine," Burke replied with steel in his voice. He would not lose her again and he would resort to any means necessary to insure it.

Algernon rose from the table. "I will offer whatever assistance I can should she prove reluctant… Regardless of what has transpired between you, I would not see her forced into marriage. It must be her choice. She has had far too many choices have been taken from her already."

That statement effectively cooled his temper. As much as it goaded him to admit it, Algernon was right. It should be Olivia's choice, and whatever it cost him, he would allow her to make it.

The men did not say goodbye to one another. Algernon simply walked out, leaving Burke alone in the silence of the breakfast room. After a moment, Burke pushed his plate away and rose. The bruising ride to Bath was just what he needed… penance.

***

Olivia surveyed the woman before her with all the outward calm she could muster. But inside, she was utterly *thrilled*. Wilhelmina Carlton was simply perfect in every way. Only a few years older than Olivia, but respectably "widowed", Wilhelmina would provide the perfect illusion of propriety.

"Mrs. Carlton," Olivia began and then paused to collect herself. "It may seem strange to many that I would choose to leave my brother's home to live alone, but I desire a certain amount of freedom in my life. Given my unmarried state, that freedom can only be had if I present an image of respectability by having an appropriate chaperone or companion."

Mrs. Carlton nodded, her blonde hair catching the light. She was far prettier than she presented herself to be.

Her hair was scraped back tightly, spectacles that she suspected were purely decorative perched on the end of the woman's nose, and her gown was the most unflattering shade of brown Olivia had ever seen.

"I do understand, Miss Dunne. It can be very difficult to be an independent minded and unmarried woman in a city full of prying eyes. I am a very discreet employee, completely loyal to my employers," the woman assured her.

Olivia decided then that she needed to be completely forthcoming. "I'm going to say something shocking, Mrs. Carlton, something that may well impact your decision to accept my offer of employment, but I must have your promise of complete discretion."

"Of a certainty, you have it, Miss Dunne."

Olivia took a deep breath. Aside from Algernon and Burke, she'd never uttered such scandalous things aloud to another soul. "I fully intend to live a life that is not chaste. If you've no wish to continue this interview—."

Mrs. Carlton held up her hand. "If I may, Miss Dunne, chastity is all well and good for young women out of the schoolroom. But for women in a position where they will not marry, or will not marry again, the expectation that they should live without… the comfort of companionship, is too much to bear. Again, I will be both discreet and completely loyal."

Olivia wanted to clap with glee. Instead, she maintained her composure. "Will a wage of thirty-five pounds per annum, be adequate?"

Mrs. Carlton lost her composure then entirely. He jaw gaped and she blinked owlishly. "That is very generous of you, Miss Dunne," she finally managed, "But surely I could not accept so much."

"Nonsense. Living in an unorthodox household should require unorthodox wages," Olivia stated firmly. "The house should be ready tomorrow. If you would arrive there in the morning to get yourself settled. I will instruct the butler of your arrival."

After Mrs. Carlton left, Olivia retreated to the music room and the pianoforte. Entering the room, she realized it had been months since she'd even stepped foot inside it and longer still since she'd played. So long, in fact, that the servants, under her brother's instruction no doubt, had covered the instrument with Holland cloths.

Pushing back the fabric, she bared the keys and let her fingers trail over them. In spite of the lack of use, the instrument was still finely tuned. Taking a seat, she settled her fingers more securely over the keys and began to play one of her favorite pieces. She knew it well enough that sheet music was unnecessary.

As the sound filled the room, a soft smile curved her lips. For the first time in a very long time she felt completely herself.

***

Outside, huddled in an alcove in the mews near the corner of the house, Charlie glanced over at Martin and smiled toothlessly. "That's pretty, ain't it?"

Martin frowned. "We should've never took this job, Charlie. I ain't got no quarrel with this girl and I don't know what 'is nibs is plannin for'er, but it ain't gonna be good."

"We did take it, and we won't be gettin' out of it. Whatever'e asks us to do to that girl, we will!"

"We'll'ang," Martin protested. "I don't want me

neck stretched!"

"Whether we'ang or whether'e puts a pistol ball between our ears, you and me's dead just the same," Charlie insisted. "Our only chance is to do what 'e asks. Right now, it's just to watch'er but that'll change soon enough, I wager."

Martin shivered. He didn't like it. Not at all. But Charlie had saved his hide more than once and he'd taken to following his lead in all things. This wouldn't be any different. Still, he cocked his head and listened to the faint piano music coming from the house. She seemed a sad little thing to him and he felt sorry for her, but that didn't mean he wouldn't put a knife in her to save his own arse. Growing up where they did, you learned early enough that you did whatever it took to survive. He could be as hard hearted as he needed to be.

"So we tell him about'er slippin' in at dawn and about the companion she'ired?"

Charlie nodded. "We tell him everythin', Martin, 'ats the only way we're getting out of this one."

CHAPTER SEVEN

Burke sighed wearily as he surveyed the account books. He'd ridden for a full day and part of another to reach the estate. Bone tired and resentful at being pulled away from Olivia so soon, dealing with ledgers and accounts were the least appealing thing he could imagine. But it wasn't about what he wanted to do. It was his duty after all to ensure that the estates in his care flourished and, in turn, the family coffers, as well.

It had been four long hours, going over column after column of figures that could only point to one possible answer. His steward had been stealing him blind, or would have had his misdeeds gone unchecked for much longer.

"He's gotten away with it for months, Lindley," Burke said to his man of affairs. "How is it possible that it is just now being discovered?"

"It's been one quarter, my lord," Lindley said apologetically. "The first month, there were excuses… tenants late with rent, repairs to the estate that never materialized. I needed more evidence and the only way to obtain it was to allow him to continue his perfidy."

"Is he aware that you've been investigating this thievery?"

Lindley sighed. "I couldn't say, my lord. I told him we were reviewing the ledgers and account books to look at ways of making the estate more profitable or to see what tenants needed to be cast off. Whether he believed that or not is anyone's guess. I did set one of the grooms to watching his cottage in case he tried to get away."

Burke leaned back in his chair and scrubbed his hands over his face. The damnedest part of it all was that he was more upset about the envisioned delay of his return to London than about whatever ill-gotten gains his steward had made off with. He was like any other lovesick pup—besotted, smitten, mad for her in a way that defied all logic and reason.

"Set another groom… one to track him and another to raise the alarm," Burke ordered. "We'll need to have all the facts before we confront him, and the magistrate…who is the magistrate here?"

"Sir John Bellows, my lord."

At that name, Burke simply shook his head. John Bellows had attended Eton with him but they had not been friends. They would not be now, either. "If it's Bellows, your evidence will need to be utterly irrefutable, Lindley. The man detests me."

"I know, my lord. Sir John has made little effort to hide his animosity… something about an old feud from your school days, I believe?"

"That's all for tonight, Lindley. We'll take a fresh look at these tomorrow when I'm not so tired that the numbers all run together on me."

"Yes, my lord. Good night then."

When the man had gone, Burke pulled a sheaf of paper from the desk drawer and penned a letter to Olivia. It would take longer than four days, of that there was no doubt. But how much longer he could not say. "Damn it all," he muttered as he set pen to page.

***

Strolling along Bond Street with Wilhelmina Carlton beside her, Olivia paused in front of a shop window. Not for the first time that day, she suffered the strange sensation of being watched. Under the guise of surveying the shop's wares, she studied the reflections in the glass, but saw nothing suspicious.

With the redecoration of the house getting underway, Olivia was taking every opportunity to be out of it and away from the mess. Shopping was an always welcome diversion, and a diversion was something she desperately needed. Burke, or more particularly his absence, weighed on her mind. The four days had come and gone, but he was still in Bath. A letter had arrived from him just that morning, having come over night on the mail coach. Much of the letter had been direct, telling her of the complications he'd faced in dealing with the problems at his estate. Other parts of the letter brought a blush to her face just thinking of them.

Amidst the displayed watch fobs and snuff boxes was an elegant cravat pin. Simple, its only ornamentation a single polished tiger's eye stone, she immediately thought of Burke.

"It's a lovely item," Wilhelmina noted. "It would certainly do well for any elegant gentleman."

Olivia glanced at her paid companion. "My brother warned me of this... that I would not be able to segregate my more tender feelings in the throes of an affair. I fear he was right."

Mrs. Carlton said nothing for a moment, but when she did speak, her voice was pitched low and conspiratorial. "Would it be such a bad thing then, to fall in love with him?"

Olivia frowned at that, glancing over her shoulder to be sure that the footman trailing them could not overhear her answer. Just beyond him, she caught sight of two rough looking men. They were out of place on Bond Street, neither gentleman nor servant. Even as she thought it, they turned and headed off in another direction.

Putting them from her mind, she considered how to answer Mrs. Carlton. Burke was to her as opium was to others. The more time she spent with him, or thinking of him, or dreaming of him, the more she wanted him. She'd always thought love to be a tender and sweet emotion. If what she felt was love, she could not have been more wrong about its nature. It was a vicious thing that twisted and clawed, by turns creating a river of doubt to flood her mind and then leaving her with such a powerful yearning for him that it was utterly miserable. Her only relief would come from being in his presence, but even then, the knowledge that their arrangement was temporary weighed heavily in her mind.

"I fear that it would be very bad for me indeed, but I also fear I am far too late already," Olivia replied softly as she moved toward the door of the shop.

It was an impulsive thing to buy a gift for him. It was something that a *wife* would do. Not a mistress. But she couldn't stop herself. Moments later, she emerged from the shop with her purchase and passed the small package to the footman to be toted along with her other bundles.

"I think I've done with shopping for the day, Wilhelmina. Let us return home now."

"Certainly, Miss Dunne. You've made many merchants very happy today."

Olivia laughed. "I will make more of them happy before too long. The entire house will need to be redone from top to bottom. If I have to devote my life to eliminating the atrocities visited on that poor house, I will do so."

They strolled as they talked, heading for Brooke Street and the chaos of a household in the throes of renovation.

"I have a theory about the interiors of the house," Wilhelmina said. "What if it wasn't bad taste at all, but petty revenge?"

Olivia cocked her eyebrow at that. "I know of no one I'd detest enough to foist that level of hideousness upon. The nude and curiously well endowed cherubs painted on the ceiling of the master bedroom are *ghastly*."

Wilhelmina chuckled. "They are a bit lusty, aren't they?"

"Yes," Olivia agreed. "I'm sure the artist, if one can call him that, intended for them to look rapturous but failed miserably in the offing."

As they neared the house, a commotion in the street brought them up short. A cart with a broken wheel had spilled crates of apples across the street. The attempts to clean up the mess only seemed to be making it worse "My goodness! What a mess this all is," Wilhelmina commented. "Perhaps we should walk further down to cross?"

Olivia nodded, "We can walk down and come up through the mews."

Wilhelmina gasped. "Miss, no! You mustn't enter through the servants' entrance."

It was amusing really, that she could be living independently as an unmarried woman, carrying on a torrid, or at least it soon would be, love affair and yet the idea that she might enter her own home through the kitchen was horrifying. With a shake of her head and a wry smile, Olivia replied, "I've become a scandalous woman, Mrs. Wilhelmina Carlton, and I do what I please. That includes using the servants' entrance when it is more convenient."

Moving further down the street, Olivia felt a slight shiver along her spine, a sense of foreboding stole over her. Looking over her shoulder, she spotted the two men again, the same rough looking fellows she'd seen before. But they were no longer hanging back and simply watching them. They were moving toward her at a fast pace, clearly with some nefarious purpose in mind.

"Move quickly, Mrs. Carlton," Olivia urged her. Her

alarm must have been apparent because Mrs. Carlton glanced over her shoulders at the approaching men and let out a cry of dismay.

Taking her companion by the arm, Olivia half dragged the woman across the street, dodging horses and carts, uncaring of the mud as they made for the mews entrance. It would be full of servants at that time of the day, coming and going from the back gardens and stables. If they could just get through the gate they would be fine.

"Run!" Olivia ordered as they sped across the street and through the gate.

They'd just cleared it when she stumbled. The heel of her boot slipped in the mud, but as the two thugs reached for her, grasping the back of her cloak, her downward momentum carried her away from them. The cloak ripped free, fluttering in their hands as she slid further from their grasp. They cursed and fled while several servants from other households looked on curiously.

Lying on the ground, her backside stinging from hitting the ground and her ankle throbbing inside her boot, Olivia considered the implications of what had just happened.

Mrs. Carlton helped her to her feet. "Are you hurt?"

"No," Olivia said. "Only shaken. What could they have wanted? Surely if robbery had been their goal, the poor footman weighted down with packages would have been a better target?"

Mrs. Carlton frowned. "They never reached for you reticule, Miss Dunne. They were reaching for you."

Olivia shuddered at the thought. "I've been abducted before, Mrs. Carlton. I have no taste for it."

"What shall we do?"

Olivia thought of Burke's letter. "We're leaving town. Quickly and before they come back."

"What could they have wanted, miss?"

There was only one possible answer—her fortune.

CHAPTER EIGHT

Burke eyed the steward suspiciously. It had taken more than a week to go through the account books to be able to track everything that he'd made off with. The man had been thieving not for months, as originally thought, but for years. It was only as the estate had become more prosperous that his thievery had grown bolder, to the point of recklessness.

"You've stolen from me, Mr. Harper. Do you even try to deny it?"

"It was owed me," the steward whined. "Under your father, I was never paid what I should have been."

"Until he died and I took control of the estate. Then you were paid all of the arrears and given a raise!" Burke snapped. "You've repaid my generosity to you with theft!"

"Please, my lord—."

"You're fired, Harper. Fired!" Burke shouted. The old man cowered before him, drawing unwilling sympathy. Taking a deep breath, he exhaled and forced himself to calm. "I'll not send a man in his dotage to the gaol, but you'll be leaving my employ and my estate."

"But I've nowhere to go, my lord!"

The cagey old bastard was laying it on a bit too thick now, he'd taken enough money from the estate to see himself settled for life. "You should be able to purchase a small cottage with what you've syphoned off... dear lord, you could practically purchase an estate!"

There was a knock at the door and the butler entered. "Forgive me for interrupting, my lord, but there is a young person who has just arrived."

"Who is this young person, Northrup?" Burke asked, taking a sip of the whiskey he'd just poured himself.

"Miss Dunne, my lord," the butler replied stiffly. "And her companion, Mrs. Carlton."

Burke sputtered and coughed as the whiskey burned its way down his gullet. He'd gulped at the unexpected news and had swallowed for more of the heady stuff than anticipated.

She was *there*. Olivia was standing in the entryway while his butler referred to her as a 'young person'. "Northrup, show Miss Dunne and her companion into the drawing room and have rooms readied for them."

The butler's shaggy brows rose in horror. "But, my lord—That is to say—she's unmarried!"

"I'm aware, Northrup," he said stiffly. "And she is a guest in this house and will be afforded every civility. Is that clear?"

The butler nodded but was clearly displeased with Burke's response. Turning back to Mr. Harper, he said, "You will pack *only* your personal belongings and you will be escorted from the estate by Mr. Lindley immediately, and you will not return!"

The older man sniffled and sobbed, but it was so blatantly theatrical that Burke was entirely unmoved by it. He rose and addressed Mr. Lindley who'd been silently observing the entire affair. "Make certain he doesn't try to abscond with anything else, won't you?"

Frustrated and disgusted, Burke left the library and headed for the drawing room and whatever it was that had brought Olivia to his doorstep. She was being reckless in a way that he simply couldn't fathom, which could only mean something disastrous had occurred.

Entering the drawing room, he stopped short when he saw her. It didn't seem possible that she'd become more beautiful in the week that had passed since they'd parted, and yet to his eye she had. Or else he'd simply missed her. He had in fact, terribly. To the point of embarrassment, even.

"I'm certainly pleased to see you, but what in the devil were you thinking?" he demanded.

She blinked up at him. "And that's how you greet your guests? Not even a hello?"

Burke glanced over at the companion. "Mrs. Carlton, isn't it?"

"Yes, my lord," the woman replied.

"If you'd seek out the butler, Northrup, he'll help you to get settled."

"Certainly, my lord," she answered and quickly vacated the room, leaving them alone.

"Olivia, you must see the scandal you are courting by coming here?"

Olivia's response was accompanied by a roll of her eyes. "Really, Burke. Did I announce to all London that I was heading straight into your arms? The only person who even realizes that I've gone is Algernon and he thinks I'm taking the waters in Bath."

"Don't be naive. The London gossips always know," he replied.

"We left in a hired coach, not one of Algernon's and we were both dressed in cloaks and veils. I assure you, we appeared as two widows in deep mourning."

"I was returning in a few days… I'm sorry I took so long!"

She cocked her head, and spoke coolly. "Surely you don't think I took such measures simply because I was desirous of your company, Burke? Really! Your vanity is extraordinary!"

That brought him up short. "If not that, why?"

"There was an incident, Burke… Two men attempted to abduct me from the street in front of my house."

"*What?*"

She leaned forward, and spoke in a serious tone. "They were rough fellows, hired undoubtedly. I've been thinking… I've always wondered that Melville was capable of plotting out such a grand scheme. The man was positively doltish. For me, this is proof that he did not. I fear that his conspirator, or conspirators, have decided to continue on in pursuit of my fortune."

The very thought of it made his blood run cold. Recalling the fear that had gripped him so unmercifully when Melville had taken her, the sheer terror of finding her in a wrecked carriage, broken and bloodied, returned with a vengeance he couldn't account for. "You are unhurt?"

"A few scrapes and bruises, but otherwise fine. I felt it was best not to tempt fate. I thought getting away from London was the best option and this, the least likely place for anyone to look for me," she explained.

She seemed to be taking it utterly in stride, and for her sake, it was important that he keep up that appearance. "And is that your only reason?"

A coy smile played about her lips. "Perhaps not the only reason, but certainly a compelling one. You don't mind do you? That I've availed myself of your hospitality without invitation?"

He settled onto the settee beside her. "You can avail

yourself of anything of mine you wish. That will always be true."

* * *

The journey from London in an ill sprung and musty smelling coach had been difficult enough. With the bumps and bruises that she'd acquired in her fall, it had been doubly hideous. And yet, in Burke's presence, exhaustion had faded and excitement, along with a healthy bit of lust, roared in her veins. She felt alive in his presence.

"I shall endeavor to remember that. Your butler may not survive the shock."

Burke laughed softly. "Northrup has never been my favorite. I'll survive the loss."

"You are wicked, Viscount Holland. Utterly wicked."

He lifted her hand as if to kiss it, but at the last moment turned it in his and instead pressed his lips to the tender skin at the inside of her wrist. She shivered in response. "Wickedness, like so many things, is better when shared."

Olivia couldn't breathe. There was a wealth of promise in his words, but even more in his tone. And while she'd only spent the one night in his bed, that had been enough to make her yearn for more. "Perhaps we can explore that topic later?"

"We will," he vowed. "We will explore many things. But for now, you must be exhausted."

She was. And she reeked of whatever musty odor had filled the carriage. "Yes. I'm sure Mrs. Carlton is seeing to it, but I desperately want a bath and a lie down."

"And if I knock at your door later tonight… will I be permitted entry?" he asked.

Olivia smiled. "You needn't knock. It will be open. And I will be waiting."

She rose and headed for the door, leaving him staring after her. She could feel the heat in his gaze. Part of her wanted to turn and run into his arms, but another part of her, certainly the wiser part of her, knew that making him wait, even if it was only for a few hours, was to her advantage.

CHAPTER NINE

The entire house was abed, except for Olivia. She'd slept earlier and now she waited for Burke to arrive as he'd promised. She'd seen him at dinner and he'd whispered to her that he would come to her at midnight. As she waited for him, she wished she'd told him to come sooner. Every minute seemed to stretch into hours.

The clock struck the hour and Olivia rose, moving to stand before the fireplace. The soft tap at the door brought a smile to her lips. As the door swung gently inward, she turned, watching him approach her. He wore only his breeches and a shirt as he stalked toward her like a beast of prey, but she felt no fear. She wanted to be consumed by him, after all.

There was no preamble or warning. Immediately, he swept her into his arms, turning her about so that she was pinned between the wall and the firm length of his body. His mouth was on hers instantly, his lips hot and hungry as they moved over hers.

No longer a complete novice, Olivia kissed him back

eagerly. It took on a very different meaning to kiss him so fervently when she understood fully what was to come afterward.

As his tongue invaded her mouth, stroking sensually against her own, she moaned. His hands were firm on her hips, holding her tightly to him so that she could feel the hardness of him, irrefutable evidence of his desire.

Breaking the kiss, he murmured against her ear. "I've craved the taste of you since I left… like a man starved."

"I haven't been able to think of anything else," she admitted, though her cheeks bloomed with heat when she said it. "I've missed you so terribly, and even with all that happened, I have to confess that I was less concerned about getting to safety than I was with getting to you."

He stepped back from her. "We'll talk about that later. We have to. But for now… There are far more pressing matters between us."

Olivia had expected that he would urge her toward the door and the stairs beyond. Instead he crossed the room to the door and turned the key. The click and the grating sound of metal against metal was loud in the silence. With only the low hum of a banked fire, the room was impossibly quiet.

He came back to her and urged her toward one of the slipper chairs that faced the fire.

"Shouldn't we be seeking my bed?" she asked.

Burke grinned at her in the dim light. "We will soon enough, but for now, we'll enjoy ourselves here quite nicely. I promise."

She had no idea what he was about but she hadn't the desire or will to resist him. Crossing the short distance between them, she placed her hand in his. Immediately, he settled himself into the chair and then tugged her forward, forcing her knees apart with his own even as he pulled her down onto his lap. For balance, she was forced to place her hands on his shoulders. Sitting there astride his impossibly firm thighs, her lips parted on a soft "o".

"I had rather thought we'd be in my bed by now," she said.

"There are as many ways to make love, Olivia, as there are places to do so," he offered softly. "If you'd be

more comfortable in your bed, we can move there now…
but if you'll trust me, I promise you will enjoy all of this
very much."

"I'll defer to your greater experience in the matter,
then," she agreed.

His arms closed around her waist and she allowed
herself to fall as eagerly into his arms as she had into his
lap. The position had possibilities, she decided. It certainly
made kissing a much easier prospect. Perched on his lap as
she was, they were eye to eye, and lip to lip.

"I take it you're beginning to see the merits?" he
teased.

"I might need a bit more persuading," she teased.
"Convince me."

His response was immediate. Hands that had been
resting gently at her waist now roved freely over her body,
touching, caressing, kneading and massaging. And every-
where he touched her, she felt the heat, that ephemeral
spark that seemed to coalesce at her core until she was
burning from the inside.

With his lips on hers, his teeth nipping at her bottom

lip and the soft sweep of his tongue to sooth the sting, she was rapidly losing control. The ability to form coherent thought faded into nothingness and her every sense was consumed with him and the delicious sensations he elicited in her. When his hands slipped beneath the hem of her nightrail, trailing over her thighs and creating delicious friction, she pressed her hands against his chest, dipping inside his shirt. She touched him with the same fervor with which he touched her.

He pressed his lips against her neck, just below her ear, "You've become positively wicked, Olivia. Wanton, even."

"Is that a problem?" she asked. It was very obvious that the answer was no, his arousal was thick and hard against her inner thigh.

"Only in that it tempts me too much. You tempt me too much."

"You're wearing too many clothes," she protested.

He reached between them and freed the fall of his breeches. Immediately, Olivia trailed her hands down his chest, until she could touch the part of him she craved so desperately. As her fingers closed around him, he tugged at the hem her nightrail, bunching it at her waist as he cupped her bottom and lifted her higher. It was an instinctive thing to guide him to her entrance, to sink her hips and take him inside her. Instinctive, but not natural. Nothing that felt so extraordinary, nothing that created such a maelstrom of pleasure could ever be fully natural.

"What sort of devil are you that you can make me feel these things?" she asked breathlessly.

***

Burke watched her face, taking in the tension of her features, the heat in her hooded gaze. Her lower lip trembled as the breath shuddered from her body. He cupped her bottom and lifted her slightly, allowing her to sink down again. The sensation of her body enveloping him, closing around him like a fist, was enough to drive him half mad. "Yours," he said softly. "Your devil, your savior, your lover, your tutor. I will be anything you require."

She kissed him then, her lips moving against his so sweetly. He guided her hips, helping her to find the perfect rhythm as she rode him. Her thighs trembled from the strain and from the tension building inside her.

The need was on him, driving him, but he held it at bay. He wanted to memorize every second, to be able to recall for the remainder of his days what she sounded like, what she looked like as passion took her. And he would revel in the knowledge that it was his gift to her. Whatever happened, even if she refused him later, those memories would be his forever.

Olivia's movements became more frantic, her cries more insistent. Her breath caught, held, and he knew that she was on the edge of release. Burke gripped her hips and thrust into her. She shattered around him, her body collapsing against his, her breath ragged with broken sobs as she clung to him.

The most honorable of intentions faded in the wake of her passion, of the stark, carnal beauty of her release. He thrust again, and simply didn't have the will to ease himself from her body as he came. Holding her close, he focused on the perfection of the moment, shoving aside guilt and recriminations for later.

It was wrong to hope that he'd put a babe in her, but

wrong or not, the desire was there. It was his best hope of keeping her.

With the weight of her pressed against his chest, her thighs still cradling his, he was replete and perfectly sated, as was she. But it wouldn't take long before he wanted her again, before he craved her like a drug. "When we can walk, we shall remove ourselves to your bed," he said softly. "A week without you has been far too long."

"I fear that will be a while... my legs are still trembling."

"And mine," he admitted. "The thought of crossing even such a small distance is daunting, but the rewards will be sweet."

She sat up straighter, meeting his gaze levelly. "And what rewards await you there that you might not also enjoy here?"

"You. Spread out naked before me, a feast of beauty for my poor eyes. And the comfort of your bed. I fully intend to take advantage of your presence here for as long as your brother permits it."

A frown crossed her pretty lips. "Why would you say

that—for as long as he permits it?"

Burke knew that his evening was about to become much more complicated. "I wrote to him, Olivia, that you were here. I had to."

"*What?*"

"Keep your voice down," he admonished. "You'll wake the whole house."

"I told Algernon I was leaving London. That was all he needed to know. I am a woman grown and I will no longer live my life asking the permission of others!"

"Olivia, if you are in danger, he needs to be made aware of it... hiding out here with me is a fine temporary solution. But he can look into matters in London to try and ferret out the source of the threat."

"He doesn't need to do that," she snapped. "I know who it is. I simply can't prove it!"

Burke felt like he was going mad. "And you didn't think this was pertinent information to relay earlier?"

"I wasn't entirely certain. I had to think about it more. My memories are so jumbled from the time with Melville. There are huge blanks I am simply incapable of filling… but the one thing I do recall was waking up in that carriage and Melville was there, but another man as well. Hurston. They were discussing Melville's plans, but whatever Melville had drugged me with initially made it all so difficult to comprehend."

"Then it appears I will be writing to your brother again," he snapped. "Dammit, Olivia. I would have challenged him. I would have called him out and put a bullet in him, had I known."

"It isn't your place to do so," she replied coolly. With some difficulty and lacking in her usual grace, she managed to extricate herself from his lap and stand on her feet in front of him. His attempts to assist her had been brushed off. "Endangering yourself for my besmirched honor is an exercise in futility. In the eyes of society, I have none. And I won't have you risking your reputation by so publicly attaching yourself to me."

He had no argument for that for everything she said was irrefutably true. It wasn't his place, but he desperately wanted it to be. Confessing that to her now wouldn't simply send her running back to London, it would have her running right back into danger.

"I won't challenge him, but if ever an opportunity presents itself to rid the world of him quietly, you can believe I will take it."

"Burke, you are an honorable man—."

"And Hurston is not. I know things about him that you are not and should never be privy to, Olivia. The man is a fiend and the world would be safer and kinder place unsoiled by his presence!"

Olivia shushed him. "Now who is shouting down the house?"

"You have no idea what he's capable of!"

She gaped at him. "On the contrary! He was the mastermind behind Melville's plan... more than likely because Melville was so deeply indebted to him that it was only hope of payment! I know precisely what he is capable of!"

She didn't. And he wouldn't tell her. Taking a lover did not suddenly make her truly worldly and the perversions that titillated Hurston were things she should never learn of.

"Trust me when I say that while you have knowledge

of his unscrupulous nature there are things that I know about him that are beyond *my* ability to fully comprehend, much less a woman such as yourself with limited experience"

The frown that furrowed her brow was thoughtful. "You are speaking of sexual depravity then?"

"I am… and I shan't explain further. It's a conversation neither of us would survive."

"Hurston aside," she countered, "my ire has been raised by your high handedness. You should not have written to Algernon without telling me."

"Olivia, I know he is aware of our… arrangement. And you say he is accepting of it, but I cannot fathom what would happen if he were to attempt to locate you in Bath and be unable to do so. I've witnessed his fear on one such occasion and I have no wish to do so again."

Her eyebrows raised then. "When did you witness this fear? You haven't spoken to Algernon in ages. In fact you take great pains to avoid him. So when, Burke, did you witness it?"

Burke realized his error then; that he'd spoken out of

turn and revealed too much. He muttered a word that Olivia had at least some practical knowledge of but was more than likely well outside of her vocabulary.

CHAPTER TEN

Olivia glared at him awaiting explanation. Every time she had questioned Algernon about her rescue, he'd answered evasively or provided such vague details that she couldn't hope to recall anything of significance. The gaps in her memory, according to the physician she'd seen upon her return, were the combined result of the drugs Melville had used to render her unconscious, the blow to the head during the carriage accident itself and the pain and the trauma afterward. Just thinking of it brought a familiar ache to her shoulder. Absentmindedly, she reached up and touched it, massaging the phantom ache away.

Burke reached out, removed her hand and replaced it with his own. He kneaded the muscles there, pressing into them with just the right amount of force. It was painful in some ways, yet in others offered a relief that she hadn't even realized she required.

"Does it still pain you?"

"How did you know?" she asked.

"Know what?"

"You asked," she said pointedly, "if it still pained me."

"Olivia, I assumed you injured yourself in the spill you took escaping your would be kidnappers."

He was lying. She'd *never* known Burke to lie to her before this moment. Not once in all the years she'd known him, but he was now and she meant to know why. Memories tugged at her. Faint, ephemeral images stirred in her mind and she spoke slowly, realization dawning, "You were there."

"I was here, dealing with estate business."

"Not the other day," she corrected him. "But after Melville took me. The reason Algernon can't tell me about my rescue is because he wasn't there. At least not for all of it. It was you."

"Olivia—."

She shook her head. "Don't lie to me. Not now. I deserve the truth, Burke!"

***

He would tell her, but he couldn't begin to guess what her response would be. "Yes. I was there. Algernon came to me when he discovered that Melville had taken you. He knew there were only two possible choices… south to Brighton a ship bound for the Continent, or north to Scotland and a Gretna Greene elopement. He took one route and I took the other."

She said nothing, just stared at him expectantly and waited for him to provide answers to her unspoken questions. "I found you near Grantham. Melville must have known I was in pursuit because he'd ordered the driver to speeds that were unsafe. The carriage was old and in poor condition and simply couldn't withstand the abuse it was taking. The wheel broke, the carriage overturned and tumbled from the road into the river."

"And Melville?" she asked. "Did you kill him?"

There was no reason to be incensed by her question. It had been his plan after all—to find Melville and put a pistol ball in his heart. "No. I didn't have to. His own recklessness did it for me. He and the driver were dead when I found them."

"And me?" she asked.

"You were still bound in the carriage, or what was

left of it. Oddly enough, that is what saved you. The position you'd been bound in kept your head above the water or you'd have drowned there." He felt positively ill just saying the words as the scene rose up again in his memory. There was little of that day that he wished to recall. Not the sickening fear, the anger and fury, or the unbearable screams she'd uttered when he'd been forced by the age and infirmity of the physician to set her shoulder himself.

"I took you to the inn, obtained a room and sent for the doctor. Then I hired a man to follow Algernon's route and bring him to us." As explanations went, it was dry and limited only to facts. It had to be. If he let her see what it had done to him, what he'd felt when she faced such peril, he'd have to unburden himself of every secret, including the fact that he was hopelessly in love with her.

"Why would you hide this from me?" she asked.

"Algernon and I argued that night," he answered.

"What about? Surely after you'd risked so much to save me, he would have been nothing less than grateful!"

Burke began to pace the room. "Olivia, for the whole of society to think your brother rescued you directly from

Melville was the better option. Being alone with Melville, then, being alone with me… it would not have gone well for you."

She threw her hands up in frustration. "It didn't anyway. Lady Haversham discovered the scandal and made as free with it as she does with her favors and footmen! But you've lied to me, Burke. You and my brother have both lied to me! I was entitled to the truth of this, whether anyone in society knew or not!"

Burke dropped his chin to his chest and tried to control his own temper. "Algernon felt it was best, and regardless of my general disdain for him now, I agreed. We did not realize at the time that your memory would be effected so."

"But you *did* know… which means you and Algernon have discussed it! And if you discussed that, I can't help but feel there are other things being discussed between you, even now! What are you plotting together with him now, Burke?"

He was caught. Well and truly caught. "The same thing I have been plotting since you were sixteen and first put your hair up… to do whatever I must to make you my wife."

***

Olivia stared at him, her mouth agape and her eyes wide with horror at the mere suggestion. "You've gone mad!"

"No. I was mad to agree to be your lover when I was perfectly aware that it would never be enough for me," he answered.

Olivia began to pace, just as Burke had moments earlier. "It's impossible. For a multitude of reasons, it is utterly impossible!"

"Nothing is impossible."

She knew differently. He'd worked so hard to rebuild his family's reputation, to undo the damage wrought by previous generations with their endless gaming, wenching and general wasting of the family fortunes. Burke, in spite of having started down that particular path himself, had ultimately chosen a different direction altogether. He was, if any member of the Holland line could ever be described so, positively respectable. Admirable even. And those terms would never be applied to her again.

"Burke, I understand that you may have some misguided sense of loyalty—some noble intent—toward me because of your past friendship with my brother, but it isn't necessary. I have made my peace with my changed position in society—."

"Dammit it all to hell, Olivia!" He practically roared the words, shouting them to the rafters. "This isn't about loyalty or noble intentions! I have loved you for ages… loved and grieved your absence in my life! I'm not some misguided young fool to be so easily swayed!"

"I never said that you were," she offered, placatingly. "But you must see that I would never be an asset to you, and with all you've sacrificed to restore your family's honor, you must marry a woman who will only improve upon that further."

"The family honor can hang, Olivia! I didn't work so hard to save the family fortune for that. I certainly didn't curb my wild, reckless and exceedingly enjoyable behaviors for their benefit. *It was all for you!* I did all of those things so that I might one day be in a position to offer for *you.*"

Those words left her hollowed out and as fragile as an eggshell. If he had, the past year would never have happened. The pain and humiliation of being ostracized by the same people who'd once lauded her would simply not have been. "You never said… If I had known—why didn't you tell me?"

His expression hardened, his eyes going cold and dark as his lips firmed. Of course, she thought. Algernon. She was, or at least Burke's feelings for her were, the root of their animosity towards one another. "He forbade it, didn't he?" she asked softly.

"No. He did not forbid it. He told me he'd presented my suit to you and that you had rejected it," Burke replied evenly.

Despite his tone, despite the carefully dispassionate delivery of those words, she could feel the pain in them. It had hurt him deeply, and while she had not rejected him herself, for years he'd labored under that assumption. "And when did you learn that wasn't the case?" she asked.

He ran his hands through his hair in a gesture of frustration. "When your brother informed me you'd decided to take me as your lover… he felt that, under the circumstances, agreeing to your terms might make you amenable to marriage to me at a later date. But he clearly has no real understanding of just how stubborn you can be," Burke replied. "I can't lie to you anymore. I won't. Because I want you to be my wife and if we are to marry, I will not have lies between us."

He would marry her. Even knowing that it would destroy the place he'd worked to build for himself in society, he would throw all of that away on her. "I can't… I won't destroy what you've built. I adore you. I always have. And if I allowed myself, I could love you, but it would be a disaster and we both know it," she said.

"I don't care," he countered. "I'd welcome disaster. Plagues, epic and biblical. Catastrophes worthy of Homer himself. I could welcome it all if it meant I would face it with you by my side."

Those words were like a knife, twisting inside her and sparking a thousand kinds of pain. It was all she'd ever wanted. She'd lied when she told him she could love him.

The simple truth was that she'd loved Burke for decades, since she was a girl. But she'd never nurtured those feelings, had instead ignored them so fiercely that they had *almost* withered away to naught. In a matter of minutes, he'd stoked those feelings back to life, building them into an inferno that would consume them both if she permitted it.

"It's impossible. You might forgive me for the destruction of your reputation, but I would never forgive myself." Her words were flat and hollow, but the conviction behind them was not.

"Don't build walls between us, Olivia, and lay the blame at society's door. I've weathered far worse scandals. Hell, I've *created* far worse scandals. That's an excuse that you've seized upon because, I think… a part of you savors the freedom of being a ruined woman," he replied softly.

It resonated within her with an unmistakable ring of truth. She'd struggled initially with her changed position, bemoaned the loss of her status in society, but in accepting that loss, she'd discovered a kind of freedom she'd never anticipated having in her life. Her reluctance to marry him was not founded entirely in altruism. That he could see through her so easily and love her in spite of her selfishness was even more proof to her that she was right to tell him no.

"I had never considered it fully," she admitted. "But there is truth in that. I've embraced my current status and I am reluctant to trade the passion and excitement of a torrid love affair for a staid society marriage."

He threw back his head and laughed. "*Staid?* Our marriage would never be that. And when we marry—not if, but *when*—it will not be a society marriage, Olivia. You will take no other lover and neither shall I… and I promise you this, for as long as there is breath in my body, you'll never need another lover, nor will I ever want one."

The promise in that statement had her shivering with need. "I've no wish to fight with you, Burke. For tonight, at least, can we not simply pretend that nothing exists beyond these walls?"

He moved towards her then, taking her in his arms as one of his strong hands slid into the fall of her hair, forcing her head back until she was meeting his gaze. "For tonight… yes. But tomorrow will always come, Olivia."

"Let it. But not yet. Not now."

He frowned at her. "I've desired you for so long, dreamed of you in just this way… your hair loose and flowing, your lips swollen from my kisses. There is nothing in this world I longed for more than to taste you, to help you discover the passionate woman I knew you would be."

"And you have done all those things," she said softly. "Isn't that enough?"

"No," he said simply. "It will never be enough."

He kissed her then, his mouth hungry on hers, but also commanding. Olivia clung to him, her fingers digging into the firm flesh of his shoulders as he swept her away with the heat of his mouth on hers, his lips plying hers with skill and with a passion that left her breathless.

Abruptly, he stepped back from her and she swayed on her feet. He steadied her, but made no move to pull her close again.

"I won't have a small piece of you, Olivia. I thought that having you as my lover, if you refused to be my wife, would be enough. But it isn't. And I won't torment myself with it any further. The next time you're in my bed, it will be as my wife."

"And if I refuse?"

His gaze became hard, even a little frightening. "Then there will not be a next time."

Before she could protest or even try to sway him, he was gone. He swept out of her room and down the darkened hallway, leaving her to stare after him as she felt her heart breaking.

***

Charlie and Martin were riding on the box, cramped on the seat with the driver while the fancy toff sat inside the carriage. When the wheels bumped and rolled through the rutted inn yard until it came to a stop, they looked nervously at one another. It was the first time in their lives that either one of them had ever been outside of London.

"Ow much longer till we get where we're goin'?" Martin asked.

Charlie sighed. "Couldn't say, but I reckon it won't be too long. 'Is lordship is calmer now at least."

When they'd confessed to losing the girl again, their employer had gone into fits of temper. He'd thrown things, heaped curses upon their heads, and then after he was done with his tantrum, had calmly told them to get a carriage ordered that could take them all to Bath.

"I still don't know'ow'e knew where she was headed," Martin commented. "You don't think'e's a witch, do you?"

"No. I think'e's the damned devil," Charlie replied. "It's the other toff, I'm guessin'. Asked about to see where 'e'd gone, I reckon. Figured she'd be'eaded to him. It's the only thing I can think of, least ways."

"You think 'e means to'urt'er?"

Charlie shook his head. "I don't think'e means to ask 'er to tea, Martin. I reckon she's a right'eiress."

Martin shook his head. "Don't seem right."

"Don't matter if'n it's right. I talked to Dottie… she told me all about this toff. We can't cross'im, Martin. Whatever'e asks us to do to that girl, we will. You understand?"

"Yes, Charlie."

There was a loud bang as Lord Hurston used his walking stick to strike the roof of the carriage. "Stop chattering and get down off that box. We've wasted enough time!"

"What are we doing'ere, my lord?" Martin asked.

"We're getting a room for the night… well, I am. The two of you can sleep in the taproom," Lord Hurston explained. "And on the morrow, with fresh horses, we'll go to Holland's estate and when the opportunity presents itself, we'll relieve him of his guest."

The two men looked at each other, both of them wishing they'd never heard of Lord bleedin'Hurston or the money he'd offered.

CHAPTER ELEVEN

The carriage rumbled over the rutted road, the wheels sinking into one hole after another. Olivia was beginning to wonder if the driver was hitting them on purpose. The sheer frequency seemed to belie the notion that it could be incidental.

A particularly deep rut tossed them about on the seat and, had they not been clinging to one another, would have pitched the both of them onto the floor.

"The roads are too bad, miss. We should turn back for Barlow Hall. The rain last night has only made them worse!" Mrs. Carlton protested.

"I know that would be the wisest course of action, but I simply can't. I do not have the strength of will to tell him no again," Olivia confessed.

"You didn't actually tell him no the first time," Mrs. Carlton pointed out firmly. "You've simply left him without a word. Though I daresay, as rejection goes, you've certainly made your point."

Olivia winced at the accusation. Certainly it was

true, but her reasons, at least to her own mind, were sound. It was for Burke's own good that she was setting him free of her. He couldn't possibly understand what it would be like to lose the respect that he'd finally managed to gain within *the Ton*. Precisely because he had achieved so much, they would be brutal to him if he fell from grace again.

"He cares deeply for you," Mrs. Carlton said and her tone clearly indicated that she believed Olivia to be dense in some way. "Very deeply, I think."

"So he says," Olivia replied and brushed a nonexistent bit of lint from the skirt of her traveling gown. It was an unfair response. She didn't doubt him. He'd told her he loved her and the true hell of it was that she absolutely believed him. She simply didn't deserve it.

"And do you care as deeply for him?

A part of her, long buried and full of hope, roared to life inside her, shouting an enthusiastic *yes*. But the other part of her, the part that had been shunned and insulted, the prideful part of her that feared his love might eventually wither to disdain like so many others, that part of her was more wary.

"I do care deeply, but who can say if it's *as* deeply? Comparing my feelings to his would be like comparing apples to oranges!"

Mrs. Carlton favored her with a baleful stare. "You are avoiding the question and it's a futile effort. You are different when he is near. Excited. Carefree. Hopeful. Happy. Whether you choose to admit it to anyone else or not is entirely up to you, but for goodness sake, never attempt to conceal the truth from yourself!"

Olivia sighed heavily and stared at the fog shrouded parkland surrounding the estate as they turned onto the road. She did love him. If she were completely honest with herself, she would admit to having loved him for the better part of her life. A question rose in her mind, one that was part of the issue for her. It wasn't until marriage had been taken away from her as an outcome for her future that she'd questioned whether it was something she wanted to be part of or not.

"What is it like to be married, Mrs. Carlton? To know that, by law, you are the property of another person with no right or will of your own?"

If the woman was startled by the question, she concealed it well. "That's a difficult question. If you've a good
husband, it's a wondrous thing at times, and at others like
an albatross around your neck. If you've a bad husband, it's
an endless misery. What type of husband would Lord Holland be, do you think?"

Olivia smiled. "An infuriating one, but a good one, I
believe."

Mrs. Carlton linked arms with her, as if they were
friends rather than employer and employee. It was a welcome gesture. It had been quite a while since Olivia had
enjoyed something as simple as a chat with a friend. "He's
very handsome. Shamefully so!"

"Yes, he is. And he's also very kind, though he'd
hardly admit it… and vain and proud. But heaven knows I
can cast no stones for that," Olivia admitted. Once again,
she looked out the window at the distant shape of Barlow
Hall rising through the fog. Was she making a mistake?
Could she afford not to?

"I know you have been intimate with him. While
that's an aspect of marriage that most brides are ignorant

of, you have an advantage there to know whether or not you will be," she paused as if searching for the right word, "compatible with him?"

Olivia couldn't stop the blush that stole over her cheeks. "I have no concerns on that score… well, I do, but of a different nature entirely. Burke is a rake, reformed on his own accord. But for many years, he and my brother ran wild together, cutting a swath through the willing ladies of society and beyond. What if I'm not pleasing to him? What if my lack of experience becomes a bore to him? In all likelihood, his infatuation with me was simply the product of seeing me as forbidden to him. Now that I am not a temptation he has to resist, he could grow tired of me. I couldn't bear that."

"Experience can always be gained and it is my belief that men enjoy giving instruction in that area… it will be pleasing to him to educate you on anything you'd need to know. And I've seen the way he looks at you. That is not the gaze of a man who is infatuated, but of a man who *loves*. You do him a disservice, I think. And yourself."

"Perhaps I do. But I can't see any other way right

now. He's asked for my hand in marriage… but how can I accept him when I know it will only bring him harm?"

"For what it's worth —and you must consider that if you marry I lose my employment, so my motives in saying so are completely pure—I think you should accept him. He's aware of your reputation. He's fully aware of how society will respond, and he seems to care not a whit."

Olivia said nothing further, lapsing into silence as the carriage pitched again just as a loud crack split the darkening sky. As the coach righted itself, Olivia recognized that it could not have been the wheel splintering as she first thought. It was gunfire.

"Oh dear," she said. "Mrs. Carlton, I fear we are about to be robbed."

The other woman's eyes widened. "A highwayman?"

Oddly enough, Olivia hoped so. The only other option, that Lord Hurston's hirelings had found her after all, was much more disconcerting. "We'll cooperate and then quickly be on our way," Olivia offered reassuringly.

"Do you think he'll be handsome?"

Olivia eyed her companion speculatively. "The

prospect is unlikely. This is not some lurid novel, Mrs. Carlton!"

Suitably abashed, the woman nodded. "Certainly, Miss. I allowed the excitement to overwhelm my good sense, but only momentarily."

The carriage was slowing, veering toward the dangerously soft shoulder of the road. If they wound up in the mud, they'd be stuck for certain and have no hope of escaping whoever it was firing at them.

"Why are we stopping?"

"I imagine," Olivia said, "that we have simply been overtaken. We will cooperate and then be on our way." How she prayed that was true.

The carriage door was yanked open and her worst fears were realized. The two men who stood there were instantly recognizable as the same ruffians who had attempted to abduct her from Brooke Street.

"The both of ye are coming with us," the shorter of the two men said.

"If you'll promise to leave my companion and my coachman behind and do them no further harm, I will go with you willingly," Olivia offered.

The man shook his head. "Can't do that, miss. The toff thinks you'll be more apt to cooperate to save'er from 'arm than yerself. Seems'e'as it right."

Olivia let out a startled scream as the larger of the two reached for her, grabbing her roughly by her arms as he hauled her from the coach. Mrs. Carlton faired no better in the grip of the smaller ruffian. As they were carted off toward a waiting waggonette, Olivia saw the coachman slumped over on the box, left for dead.

***

Burke had spent the entire afternoon in Bath. He'd gone to a jeweler to procure an engagement ring for Olivia. It was both hopeful and presumptuous of him, as she'd given no indication that she meant to accept his offer, but for a moment, it had allowed him to feel that theirs was a normal courtship and not the remarkable circumstance that they were currently in. He'd also employed a new steward, and in addition, had hired extra men to guard the estate beginning on the morrow. It might be an unnecessary precaution but if Hurston had fixated on Olivia as a means of financial support, there were no depths to the underhanded means he would sink to employ in order to have her.

It was the only plausible answer, really. Hurston and Melville had been thick as thieves and Hurston had recently become a widower under dubious circumstances. Lady Hurston, a meek and timid thing who was rarely seen in society, had perished in a carriage accident eerily similar to the one that took Melville's life. The funeral had been private. No one, to Burke's knowledge, had even seen her body. The information had come from Hurston himself and the house staff that was utterly cowed by him.

For all anyone really knew, he reflected, the poor mousey woman could still be alive. It was doubtful, but not out of the question. Perhaps she'd summoned the courage to flee from Hurston and his brutality, or perhaps the man had murdered her under the guise of an accident. Regardless of what had happened to the presumedly late Lady Hurston, he was determined that Olivia would not become the next Lady Hurston. Which meant he would have to press her.

They hadn't spoken of his profession of love or his

assertion that he meant to make her his wife. He had to wonder if Algernon hadn't been correct in his original assumption. Perhaps seducing and wooing her rather than making bold proclamations was the best way to win her hand, but it didn't sit well with Burke. Walking away from her, kissing her sweet lips and then leaving her alone had been the most difficult thing he'd ever done.

For years he'd been striving to make himself a better man in order to be worthy of her, and in one of life's great ironies, it was that very thing that might keep her from him. It was his own pride that was the issue. He wanted her to love him enough, to desire him enough that nothing else would matter. He needed that from her.

Still, Burke couldn't shake the overwhelming feeling that he needed to get back to Barlow Hall, regardless of whatever rejection might be awaiting him there. There was some sixth sense urging him on, some ephemeral knowledge that things were not as they should be.

Crossing the street to the small stable where he'd left his horse, Burke's progress was halted when two burly men stepped out from the shadowy alcove of a doorway. One held a blade and the other a pistol.

"Now, don't be rushin' off," the first one joked, flashing the blade with more enthusiasm than skill.

Burke was less worried about him than his partner with the pistol. Deciding that it would be a more economical use of his time to simply cut out what would surely be a lengthy and pointless physical altercation, he posed one very simple question. "Who hired you?"

"What?" the second man asked.

Impatient, Burke stated the facts. "You've clearly been lying in wait for me which indicates that someone has hired you to kill, incapacitate or delay me. Who was it and how much did he pay you?"

The two men looked at each other in confusion. Apparently, they'd anticipated a more fearful response.

"If you give me the information I'm asking for," Burke said, "I will match—no, I will *double*—what your current employer has offered you. It's a fair offer."

The second man tucked his pistol back into his coat pocket. "I like you better'an that other bloke. He gave us each a guinea and said it didn't matter whether we killed you or not, so long as we kept you away from her."

Olivia. Hurston knew where she was and if he meant to keep Burke from her he was undoubtedly making a play for her already. Reaching into his pocket, he tossed the promised coins to the men. "Where did you meet this other bloke?"

"The Saracen's Head. He had two other fellas working for him, but said they had another bird to hunt, whatever that means."

Burke raced past the men and retrieved his horse. He wasn't returning to Barlow Hall after all. He'd be heading for the Saracen's Head Inn and would beard the lion in his den. If he could eliminate the threat that Hurston posed, well, it wouldn't win Olivia's hand but it would at least take away the sense of impending doom that was hanging over them.

The two men watched him go. "Reckon we ought to head over to the Saracen ourselves. Seems a right enough bloke," the first one offered.

The second one grinned. "Aye. Spoiling for a bit of a tussle, are you?"

"Mayhap I am."

CHAPTER TWELVE

Burke approached the Saracen's Head Inn cautiously, watching for any sign of Hurston or the rough looking men that Olivia had described to him previously. It didn't take long to spot them— two men, one tall and one significantly shorter but both of them looking more than capable of taking care of themselves, exited the building.

"What now?" the taller one asked.

"We 'ead back to London and wash our'ands of this toff and the 'ole mess," the shorter one replied.

"Don't seem right… leavin' two women with the likes of'im."

"Their problem now," the shorter one answered. "We been paid and now we go 'ome."

Whatever else happened, Burke knew he couldn't just let them get away with their part in Olivia's abduction. Armed only with a blade he'd tucked into his boot, his options were limited.

"We'll take care of them… for another guinea, a'right?"

Glancing over his shoulder Burke took note of the other men Hurston had sent to dispatch him. They made unlikely allies, but under the circumstances he had no other option.

Burke nodded. "Fair enough."

"If it's all the same to you, m'lord, we'll take the coin now lest you don't make it back out. That bloke inside is right vicious."

Pulling more coins from his pocket, Burke passed them to the men. "Any notion of which room is his?"

"Top of the stairs and to the left. Nicest room in the place," the second man said. "I reckon he wouldn't settle for less."

Naturally. Burke slipped away, heading for the door to the inn and leaving the other men to handle Hurston's hirelings. He didn't know what he would find inside, but he prayed that he would be in time to prevent Hurston from carrying out whatever dastardly plan he'd hatched.

**

Olivia watched Lord Hurston as he guzzled spirits. The man was clearly diseased, his face distorted by lesions and his abdomen grotesquely distended.

"You, my dear, will be the answer to my prayers!"

"I would imagine that our heavenly creator would most assuredly not answer the prayers of one so patently unworthy," she replied crisply.

He chuckled. "Piety is overrated, after all. It's the penitent sinner that the lord favors."

"Then perhaps you can introduce me to one, as I have serious doubts as to the sincerity of your repentance," she fired back. "Where is Mrs. Carlton?"

"Under guard in another room," he replied evenly, placing a bite of greasy mutton in his mouth. He chewed loudly and vigorously. "I doubt you'd want her to witness what's to come... I mean to compromise you quite thoroughly. But have no fear. I will certainly marry you afterward."

"No."

He cocked an eyebrow and smiled grimly. "No?"

"No," she repeated. "I'm already well and truly compromised and have no intention to marry anyone."

"Then I shall put a blade between your companion's

ribs and you can watch her die," he stated calmly. "You mistake me, Miss Dunne, if you think I mean to give you any choice in the matter."

Olivia's stomach churned at the prospect. The two men who'd brought them to the inn and left them to Hurston's less than tender mercies had indicated that he intended to use Mrs. Carlton as leverage. It appeared that they were right. She would have no choice but to cooperate with him and the very idea of it was repulsive to her.

"So you're in need of my fortune," she surmised. If she could keep him talking perhaps he'd guzzle enough of his spirits to at least postpone his plans until she could formulate one of her own.

"A man is always in need of a fortune, Miss Dunne. Sometimes that need is more pressing than at others."

"If you'd not rest your entire future on the turn of a card, it'd be far less pressing, I imagine," she shot back. The capriciousness of it, the entitlement that they felt, both he and Melville, to completely destroy her life for their own selfish ends filled her with impotent rage. She was tired of being used at the whim of men, of being viewed as nothing more than a means to an end.

Rising from her chair, she walked to the small window and stared out into the inn yard. She could jump, but the fall would likely only injure her and would do nothing to improve poor Mrs. Carlton's position. The woman had been abducted and it was her responsibility to see her companion safely out of it.

A movement in the yard caught her eye. Burke was crossing the small courtyard, coming to her rescue yet again. She wouldn't let him put himself in harm's way for her. Enough innocent bystanders were at risk because unscrupulous men sought her fortune.

As she turned back to the room, she scanned it for any potential weapons. The most likely choice was the fireplace and the various instruments there. Walking back toward Hurston, she veered toward it quickly and closed her fingers around the handle of the poker just as he lunged for her. Olivia kept her grip firm even as she brought her elbow back forcibly into his gut.

He let out a pained gasp, but his grip on her hair was brutal, tugging her downward to the floor. Olivia got to her knees, trying to crawl away from him, but he kicked out at her, his booted foot landing against her ribs in a blow that was staggering. It robbed her of breath and her vision went utterly white.

"You're making this difficult," he sneered. "If you'd simply be obedient and do as you've been told, we could both be spared this unpleasantness!"

"I owe you no *obedience*," she ground out fiercely, though it pained her even to draw breath. "I owe you *nothing*!" She didn't have enough leverage to swing the poker with any force, but when he lunged towards her, she gripped it both hands and thrust it forward like a lance. The sharp point poked his distended gut and with a pained yelp he attempted to bat the offending item away. It gave her just enough time to climb to her feet and retreat.

Scrambling backward, she managed to get as far as the door but it offered no escape as it was locked tight and he held the key. As he advanced on her, she lifted the poker high over head, prepared to bring it down on him with all her might. His face purpled with rage and then just as suddenly, went ashen. Hurston clutched his chest as he gaped at her like a landed fish. Olivia stared on in horror as he collapsed to the floor with a loud, awful groan.

Uncertain what to do, Olivia stood there for a moment. A part of her had to wonder if it wasn't a trick, but when he continued to simply lay there, unmoving and giving every appearance of not breathing, she reconsidered. Still, as she approached his prone form, she didn't relinquish her death grip on the poker. Prodding him with the iron resulted in no forthcoming response. Olivia fell to her knees to search the pockets of his waistcoat where she found the heavy brass key for the door

Her hands trembled as she made her way over and fumbled with the lock and key. It might have been an easier prospect had she let go of the poker, but she found it offered her some measure of security as, even in death, Hurston could not be trusted.

When she swung the door open, Burke was just at the top of the stairs. He raised an eyebrow and said offhandedly, "I was just coming to rescue you."

"It seems I have rescued myself this time," she replied flippantly and much more calmly than she felt. "Although, Hurston's weak heart and dissipated lifestyle certainly helped."

Burke nodded. "In lieu of rescue, perhaps a bit of advice then?"

"Yes?"

"Stop getting abducted by fortune hunters."

Olivia eyed him balefully. "It's hardly my fault!"

Burke's careful consideration of his answer was evident in his slow walk toward her. When they were scant inches apart, he said, "With Melville, no. It wasn't your fault. With Hurston, it wasn't your fault he chose to kidnap you... but you had the means to remove yourself as a target for him at your disposal."

Olivia frowned. "So I should marry you to prevent further abductions or attempts? Really?"

"Let us collect your companion, assuming she's here somewhere, and be on our way before too many questions are raised about the manner of Hurston's death... then we'll discuss this further."

Olivia allowed him to take the poker from her and place it back inside Hurston's room before he returned to take her hand. Going room to room, it only took three attempts before they heard Mrs. Carlton's muffled response from behind the third door. Bound to a chair with a filthy cloth tied over her mouth, she sagged with relief when they entered.

Burke freed her bonds quickly. "I think, under the circumstances, it's best if we leave immediately. The inn's staff will discover Hurston soon enough and we need to be far from here when that occurs."

"Did you kill him, then?" Mrs. Carlton asked.

"No," Olivia replied. "He died on his own… of disappointingly natural causes."

Dismayed, Mrs. Carlton replied, "Oh. That is rather a let down."

Burke rolled his eyes. "We could delay our departure long enough for you to abuse his corpse if you wish."

"Really, my lord! You act as if we're the bloodthirsty ones in this business!" Mrs. Carlton protested.

"Regardless, all of it can be discussed at a later date, when we are well away from here," he admonished. "Now, move quickly."

Making their way down the steep narrow stairs, they'd just cleared the front door and were in the inn yard when they heard a woman's scream. Lord Hurston had been discovered.

As they neared the stables, Burke took note of the two men who'd come to his aid. The other two ruffians responsible for Olivia's abduction were trussed up between them.

"What should we do with'em, m'lord?" the first one asked.

Burke considered his options. "Take them to Bristol and have them put on a transport ship. When it's done, head to Barlow Hall and you'll both have employment waiting for you."

"What sort of employment, m'lord?"

Burke shrugged. "That will depend entirely upon your skills, gentlemen." He tossed them a pair of sovereigns. "Thank you for your assistance."

The commotion from inside the inn made it clear to all of them that a hasty getaway was their best course of action. "There's another stable just down the street, we'll hire a carriage there."

CHAPTER THIRTEEN

The return to Barlow Hall had been blessedly uneventful. The coachman had been discovered by a local farmer and was being cared for. The coach and horses had been returned to the Hall. Mrs. Carlton was resting in her room and Olivia was inside her own chamber. Burke stood just on the other side of the door preparing himself to go in and face her. He didn't know what was about to happen, but he had every reason to suspect that he wouldn't like it. He was going to have to fight for her in ways he'd never imagined.

He knocked softly, but didn't wait for an answer. Instead, he turned the knob and the door swung inward. Stepping inside, he looked at her, taking in every detail of her appearance, aware that it might be for the last time. "It's time we spoke, Olivia. Past time."

She exhaled on a sigh. "It is. But first, I have to tell you how much I appreciate all that you've done for me, and all that you've risked for me."

"You rescued yourself, remember?" The reminder

was uttered gently, with amusement.

"So, I did. But you came prepared to do whatever was necessary to save me again and we both know it… just as you did when Melville took me. And I cannot begin to tell you what that means to me."

He walked toward her, stopping when they were toe to toe. "This sounds suspiciously like you mean to tell me goodbye, Olivia. Before you do, you should know that I would do it all again and I would do it regardless of what has transpired between us. I have loved you for so long I simply don't know how to do anything else," he replied.

She shook her head. "You love the idea of me. The perfect girl adored by *the Ton* is simply a myth… I haven't been her for more than a year, and I've come to realize that I may never have been that girl at all!"

It wasn't just her reputation that was in tatters, he realized. It was also her pride, her sense of self. Without her position in society and without the adoration that had been so ever present in her life, Olivia was struggling to find herself, to have a sense of who she was.

It wasn't an alien prospect to him. As the heir to a

scandalous title and a nearly beggared estate, he was the opposite side of that same coin. For so many years, he'd made no effort to rise above what was expected of him, which was, in truth, very little. When he had attempted to better himself by curbing his wild ways, it had been met with, at best, skepticism and ridicule at worst.

Now their fortunes were reversed. Society lauded him for turning his life and his estates around, for he wasn't foolish enough to think that the influx of coin into his coffers wasn't an influencing factor. Olivia, once their darling, was now a pariah.

"You're wrong. My admiration for you is not dependent upon what society thinks of you, but exists simply because of what I know of you," he said emphatically. "You have always been generous and kind. You have, to my knowledge, never once struck your brother who is the most maddening man to ever walk the face of the earth, and if that doesn't speak to the quality of your character, nothing shall."

She laughed, as he'd intended, but quickly grew serious again. Cocking her head to one side, she surveyed him critically. "He misses you. And you miss him. Will the rift in your friendship ever be repaired?"

It was a subject he had no wish to discuss. The uneasy truce between himself and Algernon was centered solely on his ability to seduce her to the altar. He answered carefully. "We've made peace in our own way, though I hardly think we'll ever be bosom friends as we once were... But we should not be discussing your brother right now. Right now, we need to talk about us."

"What is there to talk about? We are old friends who have chosen to become lovers. If you no longer wish to be my lover, we will continue to be friends," she said dismissively.

"No."

She looked at him askance. "What do you mean? No?"

He planted his hands on his hips. "*No* is not a difficult concept, Olivia. I will not continue to be your lover and I cannot ever return to simply being your friend. I will be your husband or our relationship will come to an end."

"Ultimatums are hardly fair, Burke," she admonished.

There was an ugly fact that they both had to face and it was time to do so. "Olivia, I am a peer and as such, I will have to marry and produce an heir. I cannot, I will not, marry another woman and parade her about in front of you or vice versa. I cannot imagine anything that would be more unfair than that."

***

Those words were like a knife to her heart. Logically, she'd known that Burke would eventually take a wife, but the idea of it was far less palatable than she'd even imagined.

"I can't go back. I won't," she said adamantly. "Living that shadowed half life is not for me. I'd rather embrace my scandalous past and forge ahead in a different manner than to continue abiding by rules of a society that will forever shun me, regardless. As hard as you've worked to restore your reputation, Burke, I cannot allow you to destroy that for me."

"If you married, all would be forgiven."

It was naive to think so. Some would turn a blind

eye, but they would always whisper, would always wonder.

"When I was lauded by society, I refused to marry for anything but love. I see no reason for that to change."

He stalked towards her, bearing her back onto the bed as he came down atop her. His arms bracketed her head, and he held her there, pinned beneath him. "Then deny that you love me. Tell me now that you do not!"

He was so close that it left her breathless. The heat of him, the weight of his body on hers was filled with a kind of sensual promise that left her aching for him. "I cannot say that. We both know it would be a lie," she confessed softly.

"Do you still not understand why I made such an effort to restore my family's name and the family coffers?" he demanded heatedly.

Olivia realized just how angry he was in that moment. "No. I just assumed you'd grown tired of all the drinking and carousing."

"I made those efforts, Olivia, *for you*. Everything I did to restore my family's honor was in an attempt to gain a favorable enough position that I might be able to offer you… and now, you want to hang that over my head as the very reason we cannot be together!"

She hadn't known, not really… she hadn't wanted to believe him when he'd told her before. "But now that you have, I can't let you throw it all away—"

"But that isn't your bloody choice is it?" he shot back. "I'll lose the fortune tomorrow. If I need to visit every gaming hell and brothel in London—."

She slapped his shoulder with more enthusiasm than necessary. "Don't you dare," she hissed.

He grinned. "Decide, Olivia. You marry me as the honorable man I've become, or I ruin myself so thoroughly we'll have to live in sinful exile together."

Olivia grew quiet, her mind filled with doubts and fears. She feared living with him and seeing him grow bored or disillusioned with her. She feared living without him and watching him move on with someone else, someone whose arms she'd pushed him into. Ultimately, she was terrified that if she let him go, she would never again feel alive the way she did with him.

"I do love you," she whispered. "But I'm worried

that I won't be what you want or need. I've rather embraced the idea of living as an independent and scandalous woman."

"Then by all means, be as independent as you choose, and be as scandalous as your heart desires… so long as it is only with me," he offered.

"You won't mind having a less than traditional wife?" she asked.

"No, but I would very much mind having a wife that isn't *you*," he answered sincerely.

"Then you'll have to go to my brother and offer for me again," she said. "If I'm going to be scandalous, I might as well as do it in epic fashion. Do you think St. Paul's will collapse on our heads if we elect to marry there?"

He chuckled softly as he reached for the ties of her gown. "I'll offer for you again, for the last time. And in the meantime, we'll endeavor to become scandalous enough to endanger the entire congregation."

Olivia sighed happily as his fingers trailed over newly bared skin. "The last offer, and by far the best one."

Burke smiled as he pressed a kiss to the delicate skin

directly above her heart. A redeemed rogue and his scandalous bride would set *the Ton* on their teeth, but nothing mattered to him beyond the woman before him. She was finally, truly, his and he meant to savor every minute of it.

EPILOGUE

They were not married in St. Paul's. They'd settled for a much more modest affair at a small church with a thoroughly scandalized vicar and only a few intimates in attendance. Modest as it was, it had still taken nearly two months of planning. But at last, it was done.

The simple ceremony had ended and they'd been declared man and wife. Afterward, they'd retreated to the Dunne townhouse where Algernon, with the able assistance of Mrs. Carlton, had managed to pull off a rather respectable wedding breakfast.

Seated next to his bride, Burke wore a pained smile that more closely resembled a grimace. "How long must we stay at this blasted event?"

Olivia grinned cheekily. "You're far more bound by social convention these days than I am, my lord. Perhaps you should be the judge?"

He took a bite of one of the pastries on his plate more to keep up appearances than from hunger. Having Olivia seemed far more necessary to his survival at that moment than food, water or even air. "If it were up to me, we'd never have had a wedding breakfast. I would have picked you up in my arms the minute we were legally married and carted you off to the nearest bed."

She smiled coyly as she sipped her tea. "Wouldn't that set the tongues to wagging!"

"Do you really want to be scandalous?" he asked.

With her head cocked to one side, she appeared to consider her answer carefully. "No. I don't wish to be scandalous. But I don't really care if I am. I think I'd prefer to simply live my life—our life—without worrying so much about what anyone thinks of us."

"Then leave with me," he urged. "Right now. We'll make our excuses to your brother—."

"Who will be quite cross," she pointed out. "He went to a great deal of trouble. This wedding breakfast was a peace offering to you."

"I forgive him. Everything. I'll tell him that as we rush past," Burke replied with complete sincerity. For two weeks, Mrs. Carlton had stood guard, taking her duties as companion and chaperone far more seriously than Olivia had employed her to do. When he'd commented as such, she'd informed him that she no longer worked for Olivia but for Algernon and the elder Dunne had decided that some semblance of propriety should be adhered to, even at this late date.

Two weeks without Olivia in his bed, with nothing more than chaste kisses that only added to his torment. A feast for the gods could have been laid before him and it wouldn't be as appealing as the woman at his side. "Haven't we denied ourselves long enough?"

She glanced at him from beneath lowered lashes, a small smile curving her perfect lips. "I'll go up first. Follow on the quarter hour."

Burke rose as she did and watched her progress as she crossed the room and exited into the hall. Returning to his seat, he ignored the knowing smirk of Mrs. Carlton and responded to the good wishes and small talk of the guests in what he could only hope was an appropriate manner.

When the clock chimed, he rose and made his excuses. He didn't give a bloody damn if everyone in the room knew what he was about. Olivia was his, *finally*. In every way that mattered, in the eyes of the law and the church.

Climbing the stairs to her room, he knocked softly. Her murmured response bade him enter. With his heart pounding in his chest and his blood racing in his veins, he turned the knob and allowed the door to swing inward.

Olivia wore a confection of lace. It wasn't entirely sheer, but hinted at it, revealing curves and hollows but denying him the whole.

"That's new," he answered.

"I felt it was appropriately immodest for a fallen woman," she replied, even as she reached for the ties at her waist. The robe parted and fell. It was only the layers of lace that had preserved her modesty. The nightrail, if it could be called such, beneath was made of the same lace, but in only a single layer covering her skin, she might as well have been nude.

"Are you fallen? Truly? You are now respectably married," he reminded her, even as his gaze traveled over her, taking in every perfect detail. He wanted to commit the moment to memory forever.

Her lips turned in a slight moue. "We can be as married as you like, but not respectably… never say that. Madly, passionately, wildly. Those are the words I want to describe us for today, tomorrow and beyond."

Burke moved then, striding across the room to her until he could swing her up into his arms and bear her back onto the bed. "We are all those things. And so much more. I love you, Olivia. And I mean to tell you that, and show you that, every day of our lives."

"Start now. Right now," she said, tugging at the buttons of his waistcoat. "We don't have any time to waste. I'll be so round soon you won't even want to look at me."

He stopped immediately. "What?"

She shrugged, an elegant movement of her shoulders all but bared by the diaphanous gown. "I blame it entirely on you. You were supposed to prevent this from happening, but here we are, and your heir is going to be quite premature… or so we'll tell everyone. I don't mind being a little scandalous, after all, but I suppose as someone's mother I'll have to at least give a nod to propriety."

"You're certain?" he asked. It was too much to take in, too much to have even hoped for.

"As certain as one can be," she said with a laugh. When he didn't respond, her expression shifted to one of worry. "You are happy about this aren't you? I had thought you would be, but now I'm beginning to have doubts."

He managed then to shake off the fog of shock and joy and wonderment. Words were simply beyond him. So, rather than tell her how he felt, he showed her. Burke kissed her, claiming her lips with his, his tongue sweeping into the warmth of her mouth to tangle gently with hers. Everything he felt was poured into that kiss—love, gratitude, desire, hope, and utter devotion—and it was only the beginning.

THE END

About the Author:

Chasity Bowlin is an Appalachian Belle rather than a Southern one. Growing up in Tennessee, she now lives in Central Kentucky with her fiancee and their fur-babies. She continues to write gothic and paranormal Regency romance as well as writing Contemporary Southern Romance under her pen name, Seraphina Donavan. Her favorite things are chocolate, writing feisty heroines who give as good as they get, traveling and sipping a fine quality Bourbon—all of which creep into her books from time to time.